The Juggler

The Juggler

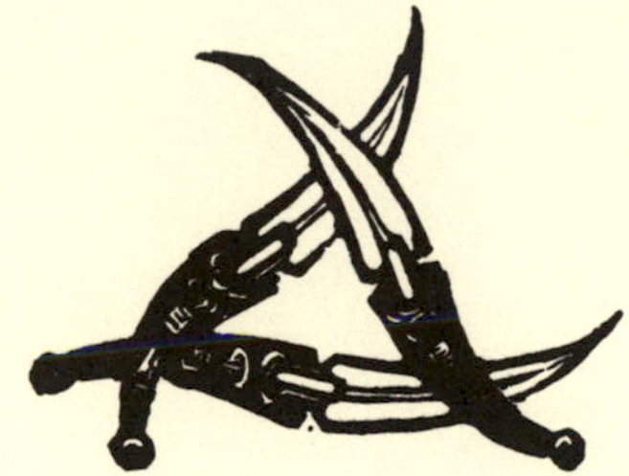

Rachilde

Translated and with an introduction
by Melanie C. Hawthorne

Rutgers University Press

New Brunswick and London

Library of Congress Cataloging-in-Publication Data

Rachilde, 1860–1953.
[*Jongleuse. English*]
The juggler / Rachilde : translated and with an introduction by Melanie C. Hawthorne.
p. cm.
Translation of: La jongleuse.
Includes bibliographical references.
ISBN 0-8135-1594-7
I. Title
PQ2643.A323J613 1990
843'.912—*dc20* 90-8070
CIP

British Cataloging-in-Publication information available

Manufactured in the United States of America

For my family

Contents

Acknowledgments

I would like to thank the following people and institutions: Ross Chambers, for his support and advice; Patricia Baudoin, Dominique Fisher, and Catherine Ploye, for their assistance in unraveling textual knots; my outside readers, for their helpful comments and suggestions; the National Endowment for the Humanities, for the opportunity to attend a summer seminar for college teachers, which helped clarify my thinking about many aspects of this text; Luis Costa, for his support and general encouragement; and last, but not least, Leslie Mitchner, for her confidence in the inherent value of this project.

Introduction

THE novelist Rachilde (Marguerite Eymery Vallette) became an instant success in French literary circles when, at the age of twenty-four, she published her fourth novel, *Monsieur Vénus* (1884). Her celebrity stemmed in large part from the public condemnation of the book: it was published by Brancart in Brussels, where it was immediately declared pornographic. Copies of the book were seized, and Rachilde was condemned to two years in prison and a fine of two thousand francs. She prudently chose to remain instead in Paris, where the sentence offered a passport to notoriety. Maurice Barrès dubbed her "Mademoiselle Baudelaire," while Jules Barbey d'Aurevilly averred, "A pornographer, granted . . . but such a distinguished one!"[1] A more measured, but no less fêted, response came from the poet Paul Verlaine. Responding to the heroine's claim to have discovered a new form of perversion, Verlaine retorted that if indeed Rachilde had succeeded in inventing a new vice, she would have been the benefactor of society.[2] Whatever the subversive nature of *Monsieur Vénus* (and the debate goes on),[3] the impact of the novel guaranteed Rachilde a faithful following. For several decades, a generation of readers and writers greeted each of her publications with enthusiasm.

Her early success can be attributed both to her independent spirit, enhanced by an unusual upbringing, and to her early apprenticeship to writing and determination to make it her career.

Rachilde was born Marguerite Eymery on 11 February 1860, at her family's home just outside the town of Périgueux in southwest France. Her provincial origins subsequently exercised great influence on her life and work. Although she lived in Paris from the age of twenty-one until her death in 1953 at the age of ninety-three, she never lost the ability to see society through the eyes of a "provincial," an outsider. (The present example, *The Juggler*, is no exception: the heroine is a creole whose marked difference sets her apart from the rest of society, and enables her to comment with detachment on Parisian high society.)

The atmosphere of the family home at Le Cros, together with family lore, gave Rachilde a highly developed sense of the gothic. The name "Cros," for example, was dialect for "hole," and Rachilde's description reveals how aptly the name fits:

> Le Cros was a damp estate around which grew too many periwinkles, too much ivy, too much Virginia creeper, too many weeping willows and too many truffles. In front of the house was a pond full of frogs; at the back there were farms filled with not very legitimate but very dirty babies. In the garden the damp prevented the strawberries from ripening, the radishes

> were eaten by some beast we could never see, and if the cows ever wandered into this garden, their milk dried up. The cherry jam was blue—moldy a fortnight after it was made; on the other hand, wild oats were everywhere, tossing their heads with the insolence of a queen's aigrette.[4]

This monstrous and fantastic experience of nature is explicitly recalled in the preface to the autobiographical novel *A Mort*, "To the Death," but it is also evident throughout Rachilde's work, in her extravagant descriptive style, as well as her dramatic awareness of the dark and hidden powers of nature. With this vision as background, family lore also placed more active and tangible forces on the stage of Rachilde's imagination. Popular local legend maintained that the family turned into werewolves once a year because one of the ancestors had left the priesthood. Rachilde's arrival in the world on a night when the wind raged and owls screeched only added to these rumors, giving her an early and personal connection with the sinister forces that would figure so prominently in her writing.[5]

Rachilde's father, the illegitimate son of an aristocrat, became a career army officer, and her mother, a talented musician, was the daughter of a successful newspaper editor. She remained their only child, a fact which was to have the greatest significance on her development. Her father had desperately wanted a son, and thus her early years, and arguably her entire life, became an unending attempt to compensate her father for this disappointment and gain his approval. Rachilde began learning to ride when she was four, and later participated in hunts, even though she sympathized more with the hunted than with the hunters, all in an effort to please.

Her need to gain her father's approval was evidently an ambivalent one, however, for at the same time that she courted his benevolence on horseback, she turned to a hobby sure to draw his disapproval: writing. At first, the activity was a clandestine one, conducted by moonlight. Later, her stories were published anonymously in local newspapers. Although writing and journalism were Rachilde's legacies from her maternal grandparents, such an activity could only irritate her father, who referred to writers as "plumitifs," making the predilection for the pen rather than the sword sound like some kind of ailment. At first, he remained ignorant of his daughter's defiance, and would sometimes read her stories aloud, censoring the parts he found too daring, unaware that the author was seated next to him. Later, he would take pride in the young reporter riding at his side and preparing accounts of military manoeuvres, but his pride stemmed in no small part from the fact that she was mistaken for a boy by the commanding general.[6]

At fourteen, Rachilde was engaged by her parents to an officer of her father's acquaintance. But the prospective match filled her with such antipathy that she revolted against her parents' will and threw herself in the frog-infested pond. Whether this action was a serious attempt at suicide, or whether the gesture was meant to convey, melodramatically, her strong resistance remains unclear, but the action made her parents realize that their daughter was now strong-willed and independent enough that she had outgrown their control. The engagement was broken off, and Rachilde turned once again to writing, this time more openly and committedly, as a means of self-expression. She was encouraged by a letter she received from the legendary Victor Hugo,[7] and set her sights on Paris. Such a goal was not irrational: for a writer to succeed, he or she could not remain in the provinces. At the same time, however, this career was one of the few available choices that would justify moving so far away from home. Rachilde's willful and independent spirit, formed by childhood experience, nurtured by an unstructured, private education, and forced into premature responsibility by her mother's increasing mental instability, could only flourish at a distance from her immediate family.

At first, her visits to Paris were temporary and chaperoned (her mother, independently wealthy, maintained an apartment there). Thanks to the connections of a cousin, she was able to place her stories in Paris magazines and made several useful acquaintances and connections, among them writers and other society figures such as the actress Sarah Bernhardt. When she turned twenty-one, Rachilde moved definitively to Paris (by now with her father's blessing), and set up her own apartment in the Rue des Ecoles. During this period, she assumed the pseudonym she came to be known by for the rest of her life. When she had first used the name, she claimed it was that of a Swedish gentleman who had contacted her through a seance, but she later admitted that this fabrication had been for her credulous parents' benefit; it was, in fact, a name of her own invention.

Wishing to remain independent of her parents, Rachilde supported herself by her writing, gruelling work since it involved not only producing the stories, but taking them round from publisher to publisher in order to place them and collect the small sum they could bring. The latent hostilities with her mother emerged more clearly at this time, as the unstable Madame Eymery attempted to undercut her daughter's career. Word reached Rachilde of a rumor that she was not the author of the works she was selling, a serious charge since no editor wanted to get involved in cases of possible plagiarism. Finally she asked a sympathetic editor for a description of the person spreading the rumors. She recognized the verbal portrait as her own mother. Whether out of malice, or because of her increasing madness, Madame Eymery appeared to believe the story about the Swedish gentleman, and thus informed all who would listen that the stories were not really her daughter's own work.

In her memoirs, Rachilde dismisses this anecdote philosophically, with an indulgence and forbearance bred of time.[8] While she acknowledged maternal disappointment,[9] she never discusses her anger at her mother. There is ample evidence from her fiction, however, that her rage went deep. There are few maternal figures, and those that exist are weak and selfish, unable or unwilling to parent their offspring adequately. In *The Juggler*, for example, there are no mothers, and maternal relationships exist instead in surrogate relationships: between aunt and niece (a favored configuration in Rachilde's work) and between mistress and servant.

Rachilde's struggle to escape entirely from the family triangle succeeded with *Monsieur Vénus*. After this success, her future as a writer was assured. She continued to produce approximately one book a year for the next sixty years (her last publication was in 1947). Although she would never again have the kind of *succès de scandale* afforded by *Monsieur Vénus*, she steadily accumulated an impressive list of novels, many of which received wide acclaim, including *La Marquise de Sade* (Monnier, 1887); *Madame Adonis* (Monnier, 1888), a companion piece to *Monsieur Vénus*; a collection of stories entitled *Le Démon de l'absurde*, "The Demon of the Absurd" (Mercure de France, 1894); and *La Tour d'amour*, "The Tower of Love" (Mercure de France, 1899), a horror story of madness and perversion set in a Breton lighthouse.

Rachilde continued to write and publish with almost obsessional regularity, and enjoyed continued success in the pre-World War I years (for example with the historical novel, *Le Meneur de louves*, "The Wolftamer," in 1905), but the rise of the surrealist star gradually eclipsed her popularity, and her later work failed to earn her the wide support of a new generation of readers. Thus, *The Juggler* (*La Jongleuse*), first published by the Mercure de France in 1900 (the year of Nietzsche's death), represents the culmination of the fertile and prolific period of Rachilde's career spanning the years from 1884 until 1900. The novel stands out as the consummation of the themes that preoccupied her in the last two decades of the nineteenth century, as well as an expression of a remarkable social philosophy far ahead of its time (Eliante, the heroine of *The Juggler*, even refers to it as a "religion," in chapter 4). Witty, dramatic and profound, *The Juggler* is at once one of Rachilde's most carefully constructed novels, a simultaneous expression and parody of Decadence, and a meditation on female power, desire, and sexuality.

In this respect, *The Juggler* continues the established and important genre in French literature of works that analyze sexual politics. It can be compared, for example, to novels such as *Dangerous Liaisons* in its exploration through an epistolary exchange of the meaning of love and passion, as well as other libertine themes.[10] The relationship between the principal characters Eliante and Leon is a dangerous liaison, indeed, for both parties, and Eliante's debt to the figure of a Marquis is not only the literal debt of daughter to parent, but the literary debt to a precursor. Eliante in turn becomes a precursor to others. With her hair worn in the style of a helmet, she is a *guerillère avant la lettre*, and a champion of women's independence. She expresses common themes of women's experience, such as the requirement that they hide their intelligence (chapter 3), the difficulty of maintaining platonic friendships and the fear that when women do act on sexual attractions, they lose men's respect (chapter 1).

The innovations of *The Juggler* are not only thematic, however, but also formal. The symbolist movement with which Rachilde was associated challenged the dominance of realism and naturalism in the novel and thus set the stage (to use one of *The Juggler*'s most pervasive metaphors) for twentieth-century experimentation. *The Juggler*, therefore, stands like the figure of Janus on the highway of prose development: on the one hand the novel turns in recognition to the past, but on the other it also looks boldly to the future.

At the turn of the century, when *The Juggler* was written and published, Rachilde's reputation was at its zenith. In 1889, she had married Alfred Vallette, and one year after, the celebrated review *Mercure de France* was born, along with their daughter. Rachilde's role in the appearance of the latter has never been questioned, but her role in the former has been underplayed or even entirely overlooked. Her name and reputation were extremely important factors in attracting contributors and readers, and thus in underwriting the success of the review. To her contemporaries, her role was evident, if not explicit. As well as acting as regular contributor and reviewer, she was the famous hostess of a Tuesday salon at the office of the *Mercure de France* that attracted the foremost literary figures of the Symbolist movement, along with international celebrities and up-and-coming writers.

One such guest was the young Colette, whose first in the famous series of "Claudine" novels, *Claudine à l'école*, "Claudine at School," was published in the same year as *The Juggler*. Rachilde's close friendship with Colette's ex-husband Willy has clouded and obscured the nature of her relations with Colette, thought to be somewhat strained by rivalry and veiled hostility. More recently, however, it has been suggested not only that Rachilde was among the first to credit Colette, not Willy, as the true author of the Claudine stories, but also that she supported Colette both emotionally and financially.[11]

Rachilde is certainly known to have been generous and supportive to another of her friends, also a regular guest at her salon, the young writer Alfred Jarry. The Vallettes supported Jarry throughout his brief life (he died in 1907 at the age of thirty-four), and in addition to material support, Rachilde in particular also offered less tangible gifts: she was one of Jarry's closest friends during his lifetime, and was instrumental in arranging for his play *Ubu Roi* to be performed at the Théâtre de l'Oeuvre in 1896, a performance which placed Jarry among the founders of modern drama. After his death, Rachilde contributed many anecdotes to the Jarry mythology. She wrote only one book of non-fiction devoted to a single author: her memoirs of the literary "superman" entitled *Alfred Jarry; ou, Le surmâle de lettres* (Grasset, 1928).

The extent to which Jarry and Rachilde influenced each other has never been fully studied, discussion having focused rather on the question of whether or not they were lovers, but *The Juggler* suggests some important points of comparison. Rachilde displays the same enjoyment of word play, in the form of puns and deformities, that characterizes Jarry's work, and shares his love of absurdity. She also shared his keen dramatic sense, and had had several plays performed before she came to write *The Juggler*. It is no coincidence that the heroine of this novel, Eliante, should be named after a character from Molière's *The Misanthrope*. The same elements that brought success in her plays—her memorable characters and a sense of timing—are apparent in her fictional works. Yet theatricality is more than a theme, it is an essential element of *The Juggler*. Not only is the novel permeated with the vocabulary of the theatre, but with the brief exceptions of the opening scene and the excursion to Leon's apartment, all the action is set in the heroine Eliante's house, with its two wings: the public world of receptions and parties approached via the courtyard, and the intimate world of Eliante's rooms approached via the garden. Not only do the two wings of the house correspond to the wings of the theatre, they even carry the nineteenth-century names for those two sides: "côté cour" (courtyard side) and "côté jardin (garden side)."[12]

Thanks to this theatrical model, *The Juggler* is one of

Rachilde's most carefully constructed novels. As a rule, she wrote rapidly and impetuously,[13] revising little, and many of her novels suffer as a consequence. Indeed, the first version of *The Juggler*, in 1900, is decidedly inferior to the later, revised edition represented here. When rewriting, Rachilde eliminated one entire chapter (chapter 11 in the original work, which appeared between chapters 10 and 11 of this edition) in which Eliante and Leon attend a performance of *Othello*. Formally, this cut simplifies the structure of the novel, preserving the unity of place (with the exceptions noted above). The excision further preserves the surprise of the ending by removing hints and suggestions that point too obviously to the conclusion. In other chapters, almost nothing has been added, and only an occasional word changed, but much has been omitted, and for the better. The rewriting removed repetitions and qualifications that either became redundant or else reduced Rachilde's delightfully suggestive ambiguity by answering the text's own rhetorical questions. The revisions leave the characteristic understatements intact, and allow a more active role for the reader, as was Rachilde's intention. Thus, *The Juggler* gained a remarkably coherent structure that gives shape to the sometimes effusive prose. Based on a complex yet regular pattern, the chapters alternate correspondence with dramatic personal confrontations. These interactions further alternate in their setting between the intimate scenes when characters enter via the garden, and social acts with entrance via the courtyard. All Leon's visits are clearly identified as occurring via one or the other of these entrances, which announce the tenor of the subsequent action.

In this domestic theatre, Eliante is the star performer: she juggles, she dances, and Leon continually accuses her of being an actress. The curtain falls at the end of each dramatic encounter (as Leon explicitly notes in chapter 1), and the plot confirms the hypothesis offered by Leon in chapter 3 with regard to the play they are about to see (a *mise en abyme* of the novel itself): a comedy that will become a drama toward the end (chapter 3).

The effect is not only to animate the plot and display Rachilde's considerable dramatic talent, but also to make the reader complicit as spectator, cast in the same role as Leon, constantly compelled to watch. Rachilde's theatre of passions evokes the drama of a courtroom where the audience-jury is called upon to pass judgement, or the spectacle of an amphitheatre in which hysterics performed like vaudeville acts for the edification of medical students. For every witch, there must be an inquisitor, for every hysteric, a doctor, as Catherine Clément notes in her study of witches and hysterics, "The Guilty One."[14] Those who fall outside the symbolic order—"neurotics, ecstatics, outsiders, carnies, drifters, jugglers and acrobats" in Clément's text (p.7), or pathological cases, buffoons and histrions according to Eliante (chapter 8)—are dangerously mobile unless locked into their symbolic position on the margins by the participation of the spectator. While Clément describes the Italian dance ritual of the tarantella, Eliante, in the final chapter of *The Juggler*, dances a no less symbolic and equally cathartic cure for symbolic illness in a flamenco which hypnotizes the spectator (Leon) and lures him into the web of the black widow (Eliante) for the last act. How appropriate that Eliante's blend of sorcery and hysteria in *The Juggler* should be situated in 1897, the year, as Clément notes (p.12), in which Freud recognized the similarities between the behavior of witches and the hysterics he was treating.

Eliante finally escapes from this circle of speculation in a manner readers often find at best ambiguous, at worst unequivocally defeatist.[15] But as Nancy K. Miller has noted,[16] the economy of female desire is often misread, and if Miller cites the example of the Princesse de Clèves, who refuses to marry the man she loves in an act of self-affirmation traditionally misinterpreted as self-sacrifice, the resemblance of Eliante to this paradigmatic character has not gone unnoticed.[17] Like the Princesse de Clèves, Eliante realizes that the only way to preserve her ideal is to refrain from implementing it, and thus her last act is committed "with a supernatural joy" (chapter 12).

This interpretation opens the way for a fuller appreciation of the social analysis set forth in *The Juggler*, an analysis which marks Rachilde's departure from Decadence and her links to other modern writers. She had experimented with themes of perversion in previous novels, but in *The Juggler* the experiment is accompanied by a hypothesis. Rachilde had been groping toward insights about love and sexual desire, but in fragmented fashion; *The Juggler* presents them for the first time integrated into one unified theory. As in earlier novels, she imagines a rather eccentric perversion with which to endow her heroine, a perversion intended to shock the bourgeois, but also a further variable in a series of experiments concerning the nature of love. Eliante Donalger is in love with a Greek amphora. The choice of an inanimate entity as love object marks an important breakthrough in this series. The vase can be sufficiently anthropomorphized that it escapes simple categorization as a form of fetishism, but remains sufficiently inhuman that it avoids preconceived notions about perversions such as necrophilia. The vase further remains gender unspecific, so that the nature of the anthropomorphism escapes definition as either heterosexual or homosexual. Thanks to the grammatical gendering of nouns in French, the vase remains both "*une* urne" and "*un* vase"; as Eliante notes (chapter 4), it can be referred to as both "he" and "she," depending on the antecedent noun. This ambiguity is deliberately preserved and exploited by Eliante to illustrate not an androgyny predicated upon the recombination of two opposite sexes as in traditional definitions, but an inclusive bisexuality based on, in the words of Hélène Cixous, "the nonexclusion of difference."[18]

In the amphora, Rachilde furthermore finds the perfect foil to illustrate the protean possibilities of human sexual expression, a theory for which Eliante becomes the spokesperson. Not only does she not need to look for a sex organ in the object of her desire, but she does not need human contact at all to obtain satisfaction (chapter 1). The "bisexuality" of Eliante's desire comprises not only gender difference; it defends the love of nonhuman objects as a natural extension of the insight that beauty is in the brain of the beholder, as maintained by her namesake. By laying bare the role of thought and imagination in human desire, Rachilde anticipates radically different theories of human sexuality, going against the grain of her contemporaries in the then burgeoning field of psychology.

Her insight goes one step further than this important recognition, however, for Rachilde further entrusts the policing of ideologically determined sex roles to the embryonic medical profession in the person of the medical student Leon Reille. Rachilde's dislike of doctors is a recurrent theme in her work (and a further link to the theatre of Molière),[19] but in *The Juggler* the problem becomes specific. Leon not only invokes the threats used to maintain traditional sexual behavior (for example, he claims in chapter 6 that Eliante will be afflicted with St. Vitus's dance and general paralysis), he believes her cure lies in acceptance of "normal" sexual relations. He interprets her resistance to his sexual advances not as legitimate expression of autonomy, but as a desire to be raped (chapter 5), just as Freud would interpret his patients' accounts of resistance to incest as a fantasized desire to seduce and be seduced. Where outright threats fail, more subtle social control mechanisms can be deployed, as Eliante recognizes. The labelling of an expression of ecstasy, of *jouissance*, which exceeds the bounds of discourse, as a "pathological case" (chapter 8) turns female desire into a form of deviance, a problem which appears to require a cure.

Studies of nineteenth- and twentieth-century history, in particular of the role of the medical profession in defining sexuality, confirm Rachilde's vision in less humorous and more sinister detail. Eliante's perception of the role of the mental health profession in demarcating the boundaries of deviance is also prophetic in anticipating the central role of female desire in subsequent theory, particularly in her answer to the as-yet-unasked question, "what do women want?" They do not know, suggests Eliante (chapter 8), perhaps failing only to add, as Lacan later would, "and they cannot know."[20]

The Juggler also demonstrates the degree to which Rachilde is aware of the role of sexual difference in the construction of meaning. For Eliante, and perhaps for Rachilde, men and women speak different languages (chapter 10). The voice—and name—of the father are internalized here, but it is precisely from this paternal prohibition that Eliante escapes in her role of hysterical juggling witch in order to speak from a different source: women write, without knowing why, just as they cry (chapter 10). Cixous suggests that women write from the body using milk and blood;[21] she might well have added tears, the invisible fluid of women's marginal status with which women write in *The Juggler*. Not "the madwoman in the attic" (chapter 8)—though a creole nevertheless—Eliante's response to the masculine appropriation of the pen is not anxiety, but an escape to a different way of signifying, one which remains invisible to those who cannot read the body. Although Eliante does not know how to write, she knows how to sign (chapter 4), and thus she is a juggler not only in the literal sense, but also in the older and more general sense of *jongleur*, "a troubadour," not just one who entertains with dancing and acrobatics, but one who tells stories, who "finds"—and signs—them.

The implicit attack on phallogocentrism includes more than just a critique of the inscription of the feminine in discourse; it also illustrates the absence of fixed meaning in language through the treatment of origins. Not only do Eliante's origins remain obscure, the origins of communication itself are irretrievable in *The Juggler*. The structure of the novel relies partly on an exchange of letters, but the model for this exchange, while not denied, is no longer available. The parable of the lost letter in chapter 8 (and described as her obsession in chapter 10) tells the story of Eliante's first love letter. Like all discourse viewed through the prism of postmodernism, including the confessions Eliante prepared with her classmates in the convent, the letter never fails to recall what one does not mean to say (chapter 8). Between sender and receiver, however, the letter fell into the sea and therefore never reached its destination. Perhaps, though, this was for the best, since the words were not hers to begin with, but literally a *translation* from those of her black other, and thus a collaborative inscription in black and white that would nevertheless remain unreadable. This reintegration of binary opposites is a mitigating factor to be set against the overt racism of the text. There can be no doubt that Rachilde was as racist as she was misogynist and misanthropic, and she does not hesitate to invoke the negative sterotypes that were all too acceptable in her own time. But the personal relationship between Eliante and Ninaude, as well as their literary collaboration, enacts a reconciliation between black and white by presenting difference as a generative force.

These themes have only become readable in Rachilde's work since the development of postmodernism has challenged the place of a unified subject at the center of discourse. Although *The Juggler* went through several editions, Rachilde's contemporaries saw little of this vision in her work, and dismissed her literary contributions prematurely. While she continued to write and publish widely after World War I, she became increasingly viewed as an eccentric has-been. She maintained contact with other writers, but these were mostly young protégés with whom she collaborated, not those perceived as expanding the horizons of literature. In her later life she became isolated, lonely and poor, most unlike the independently wealthy and aristocratic widows of her fiction. Her writing turned toward memoirs, and she ventured into (for her) previously unexplored genres such as poetry. She died in her apartment at the *Mercure de France* on 4 April 1953. Her passing was noted in the major newspapers, such as *Le Monde*, but caused barely a ripple in the literary world. Rachilde's life was both too long and too short: she lived long enough to experience a decline in her popularity and a neglect of her work. She did not live long enough, however, to witness the revival of interest and the appreciation of a new generation of readers that is her due.

Notes

1. "Mademoiselle Baudelaire" is the title of an article by Barrès in *Les Chroniques* (Feb. 1887): 77–79. The account of the meeting with Barbey d'Aurevilly is retold by André David, based on Rachilde's recollections, in *Rachilde, homme de lettres: son oeuvre* (Paris: Editions de la nouvelle revue critique, 1924), 32–33.

2. A much-repeated anecdote, but see for example David's *Rachilde*, 22.

3. In *Rachilde: Femme de lettres, 1900* (Périgueux: Pierre Fanlac, 1985), Claude Dauphiné argues the case for a feminist interpretation of Rachilde, while Jennifer Birkett in *The Sins of the Fathers: Decadence in France, 1870–1914* (London: Quartet, 1986) claims that Rachilde succeeds only in fuelling male fantasies. A more extensive treatment of the subversive possibilities of *Monsieur Vénus* in particular may be found in Melanie Hawthorne's "*Monsieur Vénus*: A Critique of Gender Roles" (*Nineteenth-Century French Studies* 16:1&2 (Fall/Winter 1987–88): 162–179) and in Dorothy Kelly's *Fictional Genders: Role and Representation in Nineteenth-Century French Narrative* (Lincoln: University of Nebraska

Press, 1989), which analyze both the subversive potential and the limitations of this work.

4. From the preface to *A Mort* (Paris: Monnier, 1886). Translated by Ernest Boyd in his introduction to *Monsieur Vénus*, translated by Madeleine Boyd (New York: Covici, 1929), 6–7.

5. Information about Rachilde's early childhood may be culled from several sources. Two works which appeared during her lifetime were based on personal communication with Rachilde: Ernest Gaubert's *Rachilde* (Paris: Sansot, 1907) and André David's *Rachilde*. Rachilde herself published a collection of memoirs, *Quand j'étais jeune* (Paris: Mercure de France, 1947), and although her novels are seldom explicitly autobiographical, much may be inferred from them. The most recent resource, a synthesis of the above materials, is Claude Dauphiné's *Rachilde: Femme de lettres, 1900*.

6. These events occupy several chapters of *Quand j'étais jeune*.

7. As recounted in the first chapter of *Quand j'étais jeune*.

8. See "Chez Dentu Le Grand Editeur" in *Quand j'étais jeune*. At the beginning of one of the chapters devoted to her father ("Un Héros de Roman"), Rachilde remarks: "One only knows one's parents when, having lost them, one reaches their age, and they come back into your mind like remorse, regrets for having misjudged them, or like the signs of a former life one was unable to understand, because one had absolutely no experience of the value of a soul always closed to another soul" (66). The explicit reference is to her failure to understand her father, but perhaps Rachilde was more inclined to be charitable in her judgement of her mother, too, in retrospect.

9. At length, for example, in *Pourquoi je ne suis pas féministe* (Paris: Les Editions de France, 1928).

10. Maurice Barrès pointed out, though in what may be taken as unflattering terms, the frequent association of Rachilde's work with that of eighteenth-century libertines in his preface to the revised, 1889 edition of *Monsieur Vénus*. This preface is included in the 1977 edition of the work by Flammarion (see p.5).

11. See Shari Benstock, *Women of the Left Bank: Paris, 1900–1940* (Austin: University of Texas Press, 1986), 205.

12. Stage right (côté jardin) was formerly known as the "côté du roi," while stage left (côté cour) was the "côté de la reine," reflecting the position of the boxes of the king and queen. After the Revolution,

the wings were renamed to eliminate any reminder of royalty. See chapter 2 of Jean-Pierre Moynet's *French Theatrical Production in the Nineteenth Century*, translated and augmented by Allan S. Jackson with M. Glen Wilson (Rare Books of the Theatre Series, American Theater Association no. 10, 1976, published by the Max Reinhardt Foundation with the Center for Modern Theater Research).

13. She habitually completed a novel in a month of frenzied writing, lying on her stomach on the floor (see Dauphiné, *Rachilde: Femme de lettres, 1900*, 48).

14. In *The Newly Born Woman*, translated by Betsy Wing, with an introduction by Sandra M. Gilbert (Minneapolis: The University of Minnesota Press, 1986).

15. For Jennifer Birkett, for example, Eliante's death is a "poor kind of triumph" (*The Sins of the Fathers*, 181), an example of Rachilde's pattern of "the temporary triumph of the vengeful female and the humiliating overthrow of the male—subject to the reinstatement of paternal power in the last act" (161).

16. In "Emphasis Added: Plots and Plausibilities in Women's Fiction," *PMLA* 96 (1981): 36–84.

17. For example in Jean-Paul de Nola's review in *Studi Francesi* 28 (1984): 596.

18. In "Sorties" in *The Newly Born Woman*, 85.

19. A dislike she shared with Jarry, who referred to them as "merdecins." See his letter to Rachilde published in the *Organographes du Cymbalum Pataphysicum* 18 (1982): 35.

20. See Luce Irigaray's meditation on the question of "che vuoi" (as she calls it) entitled "The 'Mechanics' of Fluids" in *This Sex Which Is Not One*, translated by Catherine Porter (Ithaca, Cornell University Press, 1985), 106–118. Irigaray suggests that interpreting women's silence means "subjecting them to a language that exiles them at an ever increasing distance from what perhaps they would have said to you, were already whispering to you" (112–113).

21. For example in "The Laugh of the Medusa," translated by Keith Cohen and Paula Cohen, in *New French Feminisms*, edited and with introductions by Elaine Marks and Isabelle de Courtivron (New York: Schocken, 1981), 245–264.

Selected Bibliography

Barrès, Maurice. "Mademoiselle Baudelaire." *Les Chroniques*, February 1887, 77–79.

Birkett, Jennifer. *The Sins of the Fathers: Decadence in France, 1870–1914*. London: Quartet, 1986.

Coulon, Marcel. "L'Imagination de Rachilde." *Mercure de France* 142 (15 Aug.–15 Sept. 1920): 545–569.

Dauphiné, Claude. Introduction to *La Jongleuse*, by Rachilde. Paris: Des Femmes, 1982.

———. *Rachilde: femme de lettres, 1900*. Périgueux: Pierre Fanlac, 1985.

David, André. *Rachilde, homme de lettres: son oeuvre*. Paris: Editions de la Nouvelle Revue Critique, 1924.

Gaubert, Ernest. *Rachilde*. Paris: Sansot, 1907.

Hawthorne, Melanie. "*Monsieur Vénus*: A Critique of Gender Roles." *Nineteenth-Century French Studies* 16 (Fall/Winter 1987–88): 162–179.

———. "The Social Construction of Sexuality in Three Novels by Rachilde." *Michigan Romance Studies* 9 (1989): 49–59.

Jarry, Alfred. "Ce que c'est que les ténèbres." *Oeuvres complètes*, vol. 2:432–435. Paris: Gallimard, Pléiade, 1987.

Kelly, Dorothy. *Fictional Genders: Role and Representation in Nineteenth-Century French Narrative*. Lincoln: University of Nebraska Press, 1989.

Lorrain, Jean. "Mademoiselle Salamandre." In *Dans l'oratoire*. Paris: C. Dalou, 1888.

Mauclair, Camille. "Eloge de la luxure." *Mercure de France* 8 (May 1893): 43–50.

Miomandre, Francis de. "Rachilde, Princesse des Ténèbres." *Art Moderne* 13 & 14 (29 March & 5 April, 1903): 117–119, 125–127.

Organographes du Cymbalum Pataphysicum, no. 19–20 (4 April, 1983).

Quillard, Pierre. "Rachilde." *Mercure de France* 9 (Dec. 1893): 323–328.

Santon, Noël. *La Poésie de Rachilde*. Paris: Le Rouge et le Noir, 1928.

Translator's Note

THIS translation is based on the 1982 Des Femmes reprint of the 1925 edition of the work, the first to appear with woodcut illustrations by Gustave Alaux. The 1982 edition contains a number of typographical errors, however, and in these instances I have used the earlier printing. I have also consulted the fourth printing of the 1900 edition.

Rachilde's prose is difficult to translate because of its style. Not only does she use frequent wordplay, deforming a common expression by one letter or syllable to produce new, yet uncannily familiar locutions, but her fluid style leaves much ambiguous in French. A typical descriptive passage is built up through an accumulation of phrases in which the relation of the parts to the whole remains vague. While grammatical gender in French is sometimes of assistance in determining which phrases of a description apply to which object, in many instances, Rachilde leaves a deliberate ambiguity. I have attempted to retain something of this free play in English by following her equally idiosyncratic punctuation. This calls for punctuation marks (commas, question marks) to be added where one would not normally expect them, and frequently to be omitted where one would expect them. This style reflects Rachilde's attempts to model prose after theatre: the odd punctuation and frequent use of italics suggest to the reader what intonations a line should carry, mimicking the way an actor might stress or inflect a certain word in delivering dialogue to convey irony or humor. Similarly, the use of "points de suspension" (three dots), one of Rachilde's favorite devices, is also a technique to draw the reader into the text and make him or her participate in the construction of its meaning.

Footnotes have been added when necessary to comment on a specific aspect of the text, and to draw comparisons with other areas of Rachilde's life and work.

The Juggler

CHAPTER ONE

THIS woman let her dress trail behind her like a queen trailing her life. She left the brightly lit hall, taking with her its darkness, draped by a thick shadow, by an air of impenetrable mystery that came right up to her neck and clasped it as though to strangle her. She took small steps, and the tail of black, full, supple material fanned out, rolled a wave around her, undulated, forming the same moiré circles that are seen in deep water in the evening, after a body has fallen. She walked with her head held high, her eyes lowered, her arms hanging by her side, not young in appearance, for she remained serious, and what showed above her funereal envelope seemed very artificial: a painted doll's face, decorated with a bonnet of smooth, shining hair with steely glints, hair that stuck to the temples, too twisted, too fine, so fine it seemed like imitation silk, a shred of her black dress, that satiny, almost metallic, sheath. With such a tight hairstyle set above thin red ears that seemed literally to bleed under the weight of a sharp-edged helmet, she was whiter with her makeup than any other made-up woman.

She was alive, however, since she stopped in front of a

mirror. She cast a curious glance, not looking at herself, but watching someone over her left shoulder.

The anteroom was deserted. The mirror reflected only the marble statue of a nymph holding a candelabrum over there, and here, the dark silhouette of the motionless woman, equally a statue, two twins turning their back on each other, the one very naked, spreading cold in the transparent electric globes, the other magnificently dressed, even less real, and these mute phantoms aroused the idea of an imminent catastrophe.

A door slammed; ceremonious voices burst out, chairs scraped, glasses clinked, once again, heavy silence.

The somebody watched by the woman in black was following her.

She began to descend the staircase without bothering to pick up her dress, as if no one were there, her arms inert, squeezed by her long gloves from wrist to elbow, ringing them with viperine folds, and her hands of mourning had the disconcerting look of natural hands.

On the second landing, at the point where a second marble servant lifted her spray of light while smiling a white sugary smile, the black woman let out a cry, the light cry of someone nervous who is provoked, but without turning round: her dress had just pulled tight suddenly from the train to the neck, the whole fabric had stiffened into an iron bar and the decorous costume, the chaste sheath, detached itself bit by bit from the woman, giving her up to the electric lights more naked, despite her blackness, than the marble statue. Skirt and bodice floated on her. Nothing stuck properly to this human form, molded a moment ago in its silken scabbard. This hermetic dress, the collar of which bit at the chin with a velvety maw, opened out to snatch at the neck, did not protect her from the possibility of appearing beautiful.

"Excuse me, madam!" said the voice of a man, hissing slightly.

So she deigned to turn around, to smile with indifferent politeness, to pick up her train, with one sweeping gesture, like someone picking up the handle of a basket full of flowers.

She was so supple, she bent over so quickly that, suddenly, one guessed she was younger, more *animal*, perhaps more lighthearted, capable of running.[1]

She raised her skirt, she raised her eyes; one could see her feet, hardly covered by an edging of leather that matched her gloves, naked and black feet in lace stockings; one could see her eyes, naked and black beneath a silky fringe of bits of fur.

The man stopped hypnotized, short of breath.

He had trodden on the skirt because he could see nothing but the woman.

She continued, descended majestically, became serious once more.

At the last landing and at the third marble servant, the cloakroom attendant gave her an evening wrap, an indescribable thing in which pearls clicked with sabre blades. Her frail black hands quickly got the better of the immense oriental stole; she draped herself with the few movements of a cat getting under the bedcovers, and very carefully veiled her lips, probably afraid of coughing.

The man who had stopped up there reached the cloakroom attendant, asked for his overcoat, a simple overcoat of poor cloth, and he again mechanically followed the wake of luminous silks as they were swallowed by the night of the street after having masked the night of the woman.

His destiny drove him after the black train. He would not go far, for he knew that she had her carriage, a low coupé, a small dark box in which the glittering toy would faint, return home abruptly, extinguish her magic glow. And that had been exasperating him for a long time.

She always wore black: a serious woman.

She had a discreet carriage: a rich woman.

But she deployed, at the end of these monotonous official evenings, a violent stole, an adventurer's stole, like a firework. He would feel himself irresistibly drawn to a conquest that seemed possible, if not easy, then she would take off at the gallop of a great infernal horse, a legendary horse.[2]

He was not unaware of her name and address. She was called Madame Donalger, and lived in an old house in a new neighborhood, in the direction of the Trocadéro.

He knew her first name, too: *Eliante*. He found it quite ridiculous.

. . . And charming!

Someone had introduced him that very evening. Some gentleman muttering:

"You should escort madam to the buffet. She doesn't want to go alone."

Why? Did she never know anyone, then? And in escorting her to the buffet, in actually shivering with anxiety at feeling her so black, so closed up, he had said nothing to her.

Once, at a certain Baronness d'Esmont's where he had slipped in, as always to follow her, he found her dance card under her chair, with cards, her own, and he finally read this first name: *Eliante*, and that made him sneer a little:

"That's all I need! She's called *Eliante*."[3]

And still laughing to himself, he took a card, stole it, kept it, to reread it in the morning.

"Who can she be, that woman?"

It was not enough for him that it was a woman.

Now he was hurrying into the street, not waiting for the end of the party, his head uncovered in the pouring rain.

"It's raining. Damn it all!"

Stuck in the middle of the sidewalk, not thinking to put on his crush-hat because he would have to unfasten the spring and he dreaded such a noisy complication, he cursed.

The coupé was standing in front of him.

She was getting into the carriage, arranging the black cascade of the dress, the multicolored waves of the coat, causing light, very white petticoats to gush out, like champagne bubbles.

The man was shaking with rage.

He felt such a strong desire to go up to her, such a brutal urge of instinct, that he took several more steps in spite of himself; he plunged his polished shoes into a mud puddle, reached the carriage door, put his hand on the handle, firmly resolved to prevent the horrible box from closing, to ravish its toy.

At that very moment, the man was split, he wanted, on the one hand, quite frantically *to look at her* again and, on the other hand, he was mentally calling himself a fool, thinking that she would give him some spare change, as one does to street urchins who run up to the carriage windows.

The woman drew aside the silk veiling her mouth, and she asked, quite naturally:

"Would you like to get in, my dear sir?"

Would he like to get in? Good heavens! His instinct alone answered. He bounded, settled into the dark silks, scattered the oriental lights, ravaged, with his muddy feet, the underlying foam, sat down and gestured in vexation:

"Excuse me, madam! Please accept my apologies," he said, dazed by his own audacity, "I'm nothing but a fool, indeed. I step on your dress, I get into your carriage . . . I'm losing my head. What's more, I have a migraine, these evening dances aren't good for me. I beg you, excuse me, I'll get out."

She burst out laughing, a very open laugh, very girlish, throwing her head back a little to hide the real expression of her gaiety.

The coachman, perplexed, waited for an order.

So she stifled the desire to laugh, put on the serious expression of a protective matron:

"Drive on, Jean, drive on! I'm taking the gentleman home with me."

And the carriage moved off, with the trot of a great infernal black horse, the black horse of the legends.

Incredibly, they exchanged banalities during the journey.

"What terrible rain!" murmured the woman, pulling at the end of her gloves, which gave her pointed claws. "You would think it was the flood; it's been going on for three days."

"It's quite wretched weather. We're having an awful end of autumn."

"Quite a fine affair, eh, for a charity ball? Very ingenious buffet decorations, those fountains of wine and those white bouquets. So you don't like dancing, sir?"

"Me? I don't know how to dance."[4]

"You were at the Baronness d'Esmont's on Thursday. Yet it was a ball."

"I went . . . without realizing."

"You often go *without realizing*, don't you, sir?"

And he tried to stare her down, to be bold, even to act as though he had struck lucky, only he felt paralyzed, made awkward, by the terror that he would be thrown peremptorily out of the carriage and the quite tenacious desire to remain before her, sitting on the end of her oriental stole.

She murmured:

"I left early because . . . I'm hungry. The buffet . . . very elegant, but did you get a close look at those sandwiches? Disgusting! Just bread and butter! They smelled of rancid ham. I'll have supper at home, I'll be better off."

He grumbled:

"I must seem extremely coarse, madam?"

"Not at all, on the contrary. I'm sure you are a very well brought-up man, and that's why I'm inviting you to come and share my supper."

"Madam, it would be more natural that I invite you."

"Oh! *That you invite me*! Admirable use of the subjunctive. No . . . don't you dare do anything of the kind, I beg you, I would be hurt. I am quite entitled to receive you—I am your elder,—to treat you like a little boy in disgrace. You leave, *without realizing*, a very merry party, and I'm punishing you by taking you home to a lady in a sad mood." (She was laughing the whole time.) "I'm sad, you know, because I suffer."

"Are you ill? What's the matter?"

"I'm suffering . . . from spleen, because of the rain, because of the autumn."[5]

"I say, don't make fun."

"I could be even more unkind. After all, have I asked you for your address?"

"You saw me stealing one of your cards?"

"You weren't very clever, you were doing it in front of everyone, sir."

Violently, he snarled:

"I'm not in love with you . . . in case I look it! I'm not going to fall for any woman. No, never. You look like a curious object to me, and I find it amusing to look at you close up . . . in the shop window. Don't want to touch . . . nor to buy, I assure you."

A short silence fell like hail. The woman coughed lightly.

"Buy?" she sighed. "Poor child!"

He shuddered. She had said this in an emotional voice, deliciously maternal. The insult hardly touched her. She was feeling sorry for the very person who was trying out, on her, his brand new male cruelty.

"You take me for a child. I'm of age, madam. I'm twenty-two years old."

"And I, sir, am thirty-five."

He clenched his fists, furious, without knowing why.

"More like forty," he thought.[6]

"I'm not lying," she added, though he had said nothing.

"You pass by, you look at me and I accept it. Admit that I would have the right to lie to you, if I wanted to."

"Wait, madam, let me out. Let's go our separate ways, as befits people not made for each other. Only. . . . Prove to me that you are not a negress!"

He forced a laugh.

She took off her glove and held out her hand.

It was a very small hand, and very powerful, in spite of its frail appearance, with thin fingers, short nails, slightly furrowed knuckles, a voluptuous palm that clung like a limpet, but this hand, without rings, flashed with whiteness, and exuded a penetrating perfume, a peppery, acidic odor, the name of which would not come to mind at once, even if you savored it, a smell of island fruit.

"Oh! madam," stammered the young man contemplating this hand by the fleeting light of the lanterns, "you spoil me!" (He was examining this pretty piece of flesh with the eyes of an expert in the art of discovering physical flaws.) "Yes," he said seriously, "you must be suffering, ill, or distressed, an ether drinker, or a morphine addict, or . . . the heart . . . The blue veins along your wrist . . . are almost violet and . . . it's exquisite."

"Not as ill as that. I'm bored, that's all. As for you, you're a medical student."

She smiled.

He shrugged.

"No doubt; quite a poor . . . little boy. I'm bored, too. That luxury is the only thing we have in common, madam."

"Oh! It's quite enough to make us both rich. . . ."

The carriage came to a halt.

They had to venture out into the dismal night once more with the rain beating on their backs.

The coachman opened the door, then a gate in front of the carriage, the wet branches causing a sudden downpour.

"Don't make any noise, dear sir, I have a child sleeping in the house. That's why the carriage turned in through the garden. Are you there?"

"Yes, madam, and yet . . . it would have made more sense to go somewhere else for supper . . . don't you think? so as not to wake your . . . child."

"She's not my daughter, she's my niece. And then there is my old brother-in-law, too. He is deaf, fortunately! No, I prefer to have supper at home."

So, as she went up the front steps, she took his arm, pushed him, guided him past the boxes of large, humid plants.

"There . . . we've arrived," she whispered. "I live on the ground floor, the others are above."

"That's wise," he retorted.

They found themselves in a round dining room, lit by a huge yellow tulip, that bloomed over a delicately set table at a touch of Eliante's forefinger.

One single place setting, but two partridges, two pitchers of cream, two dishes of fruit and gateau,—the gateau, in strange shapes, the fruit, superb—It was warm; green silk hangings trickled in wavy folds from the ceiling like weeping willow branches, shelves held crystalware in varied, and fluid, shades, neither door, nor window was visible, and a thick carpet, as soft as grass, imprisoned the ankle. It might be described as a bit of summer garden at dusk, a corner of warm garden, all silvery with reflected moonlight.

"Not anticipating that I would have the pleasure of inviting you back, dear sir, only one place has been set. Allow me to double it. I don't like servants while I'm eating. How about you?"

This was said with somewhat heavy irony. He let her organize a second place setting without answering.

She sat down, throwing her heavy oriental coat over the back of her chair, a cathedra of reddish wood, naively carved, a very old seat, enormous and solid.

"There, we're comfortable, we'll eat a lot, and drink a little; and then you'll be so kind as to leave by the way you know. The gate is still ajar. But take off your overcoat, Mr., Mr . . . what was it again? I forgot. . . ." (And she pinched her lips together, mockingly.) "Introduce yourself."

"Leon Reille, madam."

"Perfect: *Leon Reille, my best friend.* I remember the commissioner saying that at the buffet, the tall one with the stupid look. Are you really his best friend?"

"Me? It's the second time I've met him."

"Ah! So much the better."

And they burst out laughing.

She cut up the partridges, her hands freed from their black sheaths, her torso snugly pressed into the scabbard of her dress, and only her white hands were clearly visible, seeming even more naked. She was decidedly made-up, very pale from either powder or complexion. Even her eyes, black and white, were hidden beneath the fur of her eyelashes. Nothing showed her to be a woman. She remained a large, painted doll, very interesting because it is perfectly natural for dolls to be artificial.

Could one play with that doll?

She ate with a hearty appetite, mixing things on her plate: slices of banana and truffles, she spread cream on sandwiches, drank out of an unusual, crescent-shaped glass, in which the wine, or perhaps water, changed shade each time she took a drink.

She seemed at once very much at home and outside of all possible worlds.

He ate a lot to give himself something to do, drank little, fearing to displease her and felt acutely uncomfortable.

The light which fell directly on him made him younger, almost schoolboyish. He was dark-haired and clean-shaven, with a hard, stubborn chin, a straight nose, flaring slightly at the nostrils, dark grey eyes that seemed to be searching, scouring, dreaming, and as though veiled with a bluish film, a transparent curtain drawn across the passions that lay dormant deep down within him. He moved awkwardly in his black suit and did not know how to tie the difficult knot of his cravat properly.

For an instant, during desert, the young man's feet lightly brushed those of Madame Donalger.

He pulled back, embarrassed, for he knew they were covered with mud.

"How vulgar you must find me," he murmured.

"No, I find you *natural*, which surprises me, with all the artificial young people running around these days. And that's why you're here."

"I quite understand. Do you think I'm naive?"

She examined him for a moment. Her black eyes caught one of the golden flames of the tulip. She put an elbow on the table, cupping her cheek in her palm. She thought for a moment, maintaining a grave expression. When she laughed, she had an extraordinary little-girl face. When she became serious again, she assumed a tragic mask.

"I see you," she said finally, "as you will be, if not as you are, dear sir. You're trying in vain to resist the *god* who leads you; only the *god* is stronger than you are, and he will play some nasty tricks on you. No, I never make fun of those whom a *god* deigns to lead. I wouldn't dare."

"The god . . . is it you?"

"I'm only a woman, nothing more . . . nothing less," she added with quiet pride.

"Good. And the temple?"

She did not answer, serious still.

He lowered his head, biting his lips, regretting his answer and vexed at not being able to find something wittier or more direct.

Around him, the deep silence, the warm atmosphere dulled his thinking. He had the feeling of sinking down into a comforter. The crystal glass cast trembling rays of moonlight, the silverware, light to handle, clinked discretely against the delicately colored porcelain, rousing only his appetite, and when he drank, the bouquet of the wine gave him the illusion of chewing flowers.

He softened.

"I think you're a good person. At first you frightened me. Now I'm not afraid . . . except of your dress. You should take it off, it's too black."

"I never take off dresses, sir."

"Do you sleep in them?"

Disdainfully, she offered him the two creams: one green, one pink.

"Pistachio or raspberry, dear sir? You have my permission to mix them as I intend to do myself, and then here is powdered vanilla, ginger, Indian pepper and grated spices. What would you like? It's a Chinese system."

She fiddled with some small silver utensils, microscopic salt cellars decorated with precious cabochons, that gleamed under her pale fingers, and she scooped out powders as dark as ashes.

"I'll try everything, of course. Only it's terrible, your Chinese system. Vanilla, ginger, Indian pepper! That's enough to set a harem ablaze . . . including the eunuchs! And you claim that you're only a woman? Indeed!"

"Here, a little of this brown liqueur . . . three drops. It's essence of tea, which unifies all the other flavors, adds just a hint of bitterness. Do you like that?"

Leon Reille made a grimace of willingness.

"Have to get used to it . . . I would prefer . . ." (He stared at the Turkish crescent, her glass, which she was raising to her mouth.) ". . . the three drops of what is left in your glass. It's so strange, that receptacle. It must be difficult to drink out of."

She held it out to him graciously.

So he turned pale.

"Do you really mind?"

"What's to risk? My glass is full of pure water."

"Oh, really," he growled, thickly.

"I'm telling the truth.[7] Drink it, it will clear your chest."

He seized the glass, a small vessel with a twisted stem and a disc-shaped bowl, and tried to adjust his lips to it.

"Not there," cried Madame Donalger, gaily. "The other side. No! No! Not in the middle. As if you were drinking oil from an ancient lamp, a wick-lamp! oh, how clumsy!"

Leon Reille had just smashed the glass by knocking it against his furious teeth.

"My apologies," he said, wiping his bleeding lower lip.

"I don't know how to go about it. So it's your fault, you should have helped me."

She laughed very innocently.

"There! I warned you, dear sir . . . pure water, and it's not good, with the Chinese system."

"Oh! You are exasperating, you are, above your black dress!"

And suddenly he was standing behind her chair.

"I beg you, take it off, that dress, Madame Eliante . . . or throw me out of the house immediately. Loosen it, just a little. Unfasten the neck, it seems as though you are suffocating. Anyone would think you were living inside a snakeskin. Personally, it gives me the chills . . . as for you, it must make you too hot."

With a quick gesture, she wrapped herself up in her big oriental stole.

"But I'm an old woman, and I'm afraid of catching a cold in the head, dear sir."

She laughed, unperturbed, as she continued to measure out nice little mixtures, vanilla, ginger, pepper, raspberry cream and pistachio cream, she stirred the pungent powders, tasting them on dainty little gold spatulas.

Leon Reille watched her anxiously. Gradually, his eyebrows met in a frown. She was making fun of him, that was becoming clear.

"Listen here, you insolent woman," he muttered, taking her nervously by the shoulders. "I don't think I love you, because I have no desire to coo like smitten lovers are supposed to. I want you, that's all. I will have you, that's for sure . . . as sure as you are an odious flirt . . . or a madwoman. I've been following you for three months, sometimes through salons where I twiddle my thumbs and get so bored I could scream, other times in the street, when you go out on foot . . . in other words not very often. I've been honorably discreet, I tried to chat this evening, after our solemn introduction at the buffet, back there. I have nothing to say to you, socially speaking. I'm not good at lying . . . and I think I'm your equal. Give me what I want and then throw me out, that will be fine with me. I probably will not come back. But don't poison me any more with your pretty little systems. You'll end up making me drink crushed glass. Thank you very much, but I'm not in a Chinese mood, and this kind of torture is getting on my nerves for nothing. I warn you that I'm not an agreeable young man. I'm not asking if you love me. Don't give me your heart, sick or healthy, my proud, beautiful madame, politeness aside, I would forget it between the pages of my medicine book, I would crush it. I have a hatred for all women, for I suspect they are malicious. A bit of luck, isn't it, when you meet one who isn't totally stupid! I like you, you like me . . . so why all the faces? You *picked me up* on the street in the most absolute sense . . . yes, madame, the way a prostitute picks up a trick. What do you want, in exchange for what I'm asking? The evening when I stole one of your cards right in front of you, to find out your name finally, you should have forbidden me to follow you . . . Eliante! What a strange name! It's crazy to be called that!"

By now he was holding her wrists, her thin wrists where fine, little vipers of an almost violet blue, could be seen twisting under her tender, white flesh.

"Eliante?"

She stood up, letting slip the multicolored shawl, her flag of adventure, and seemed blacker, taller:

"Now it's my turn, listen to me, my . . . dear child . . . and don't hurt me for nothing. I'm free to choose the time and even to not want to at all. I'm capricious, bored, in enough pain to fear an increase of physical or moral suffering. I seek only peace and oblivion. You have come to keep me company thus far . . . honorably. You will return . . . without me. Such things happen in the best of worlds. One has supper and retires. I find it absurd that a man cannot have an intimate chat with a woman . . . even one he loves. I receive you as my guest in fact because I like you . . . so what?"

"An actress!" he sneered. "I know the farce I am supposed to act; throw myself on my knees and swear that I'm happy! Never. I can't. I'm drawn to you by a different curiosity from the one that draws little snobs. I'm not amused by the manners of *high society where one is bored*. Here, Eliante, I'm going to confess to you my real curiosity, the idea of a future doctor of medicine. I think you have leprosy, I'm taking exact note of your malady, heart or head, and now I'll retire very properly."

He was trying to joke, but he was beginning to want to bite her.

Her resistance was too absurd. What did she want from him?

"Give me your arm, and let's go into the salon," she said, starting to smile.

He obeyed mechanically *because he was wearing a suit*; if he had been in an ordinary jacket, he would undoubtedly have raped her.

The French, those of true French blood, have these sudden moments of respect for the clothes they are wearing and are very sorry for it later.

Eliante moved aside a green drapery that slipped through her hands like moving foliage.

They went into the salon.

It was a boudoir hung in old rose crêpe, a soft material, garlanded with Bengal lights of Venetian glass which lit up as soon as they crossed the threshold. The furniture seemed fragile, also of crystal. Among the strange knickknacks of Japanese complication or Chinese tortuousness, there was one admirable objet d'art placed in the middle of the room on a pedestal of old rose velvet, like an altar; an alabaster vase the height of a man, so slim, so slender, so deliciously troubling with its ephebe's hips, with such a human appearance, even though it retained the traditional shape of an amphora, that the viewer remained somewhat speechless. The foot, very narrow, like a spear of hyacinth, surged up from a flat and oval base, narrowed as it rose, swelled, at mid-height, to the size of two beautiful young thighs hermetically joined and tapered off towards the neck where, in the hollow of the throat, an alabaster collar shone like a fold of plump flesh, and, higher up, it opened out, spreading into a corolla of white, pure, pale convulvulus, almost aromatic since the white, smooth material with its milky transparence had such lifelike sincerity. This neck spreading into a corolla made one think of an absent head, a head cut off or carried on shoulders other than those of the amphora.

"What a marvel!" cried Leon, completely seduced by this apparition of the adorable chastity of line.

"Isn't it beautiful! Isn't *he* beautiful," continued Eliante feverishly. "Oh, he is unique. It's impossible to think of anything more charming. You would think, when the light penetrates it obliquely, that it's inhabited by a soul, that a heart burns in this alabaster urn! You were telling me about pleasure? This is another thing entirely! This is the power of love in an unknown material, the madness of silent delight. He will never say anything. He is very old, centuries old, he has stayed young because he has never cried his secret to anyone." (She came and wrapped her black arms around the amphora's neck.) "Look closely, and try to see for a moment . . . through my eyes! Come and touch. I give you permission. . . . Go very gently, too firm a caress would tarnish it." (She seized the young man's hand and moved it carefully over the innocent whiteness of the vase, its virgin's flanks.) "Feel, can't you, that hopeless softness of the curve finally delineated? It won't go any further, for it has reached perfection. It will neither grow nor diminish, it is beauty immutable. Ah, I really want you to know, for at least five minutes, how to be in ecstasy, the right way and over something immortal. You're not laughing any more? It makes you afraid, it makes you ashamed! Oh! I knew quite well you were very intelligent . . . because pleasure turns you pale. This miraculous vase is pale with the pleasure of being itself! It has no history. I obtained it through the usual intermediaries, I was going to say *procurers*! Someone sold it to me in Tunis the way they would have sold a slave. It had been discovered in the excavations. . . . Which excavations? I don't know . . . and it was broken, but I had it . . . *taken care of*, the old wound is invisible. It doesn't have a handle. It would be horrible to think his arms had been immobilized forever. And it has no jewel, no inscription, no little dog collar, coral beads or gold Greek bands. I love it for its total innocence. . . . And the things he has seen, good heavens? Terrifying things, no doubt, underground, plunged into darkness, for centuries! He will never tell, but he knows . . . this charming body in which life has been replaced by perfume, by wine . . . or by blood! . . . . —Perhaps they just pickled olives in it, after all!—I paid very little for it, considering its unique beauty. He is mine. I had this little chapel built for him, but it's too modern. Nothing here reminds him that he was ever anything but a statue . . . I regret it. I would have liked to surround him with sacred objects. I want him to be protected from the sun's gaze, I screen him from the daylight so that he can dream in the darkness and silence to his hermetic heart's content. Do you understand, I love him!" (She bent her head over the open neck, and, inhaling with all her might, she appeared, suddenly, to become the living head of the insensate body.) "I pour in rare essences, rose leaves, I threw a ring in there. Sometimes I amuse myself by adorning him with my diamonds, or putting a chain of fresh violets around him . . . and I kiss him, and imagine he's happy. Perhaps he's offended? Do you understand what I'm trying to tell you?"

Leon Reille looked at her with superstitious admiration. He was gaining, for this woman, the respect of a young *savant* already in love with forms, colors, everything that recalled the power of the grace and principal beauty of his life: art, its transposition into the eternal. Yes, certainly, he found that more interesting than the society woman's cackling. If she loved pretty objects to this extent, it was because she had a very highly developed artistic sense; but, as she continued to caress the hips of the alabaster vase, having released the hand of the sensual man, the man madly sensual, to the point of being shy, he winced.

"Leave that alone," he said to her softly. "You're a wretched fanatic, worshipping yourself in what is, in the end, a base material. Alabaster is a product of the earth which, without the men who sculpt it, would remain . . . earth. . . .

It would be more charitable to pay attention to your *best friend* of one evening and give him the favors you are giving to this senseless character. Believe me, my dear, one is in love only with oneself . . . that's why more than two can never love decently. Let's not waste time flattering marble. Eliante! My word, your hands are clammy! You are livening up and you seem to be living in honor of . . . this pot?"

The young woman, her eyes half closed, clung more tightly to the neck of the amphora. She pressed both arms around the collar of the stone flesh, and leaned over the corolla of the opening, kissing the void:

"No! No! You don't understand me at all . . . but I like you enough to explain. I am truly in love with everything that is beautiful, good, that seems absolute, the very definition of pleasure. But pleasure is not the goal; it's a way of being. Me, I'm always . . . *happy*. I wanted to bring you here to show you that I don't need a human caress to reach orgasm. . . . It's enough for me to be . . .—don't squeeze my arm like that—for I carry within myself the secret of all knowledge by knowing simply *how to love*. I'm disgusted by union, which destroys my strength, I find no delightful plenitude in it. For my flesh to be roused and to conceive the infinity of pleasure, I don't need to look for a sex organ in the object of my love! I am humiliated because an intelligent man immediately thinks of . . . sleeping with me. . . . Tomorrow you would love me no longer . . . if you love me as little as that. Indeed, you don't love me, sir. So what do you claim to be offering me? What confidence can one have in this man who is just passing through? You won't pass through my house . . . or you will stay. A thrill? That is not much for someone who is one living thrill! A flame? That is too little for someone who is a whole furnace! My malady? I admit it: I'm dying of love and, like the phoenix, I am reborn, after burning up, with love! Quite simply. It's no more surprising than that, even though it surprises all the doctors. No, I never take off my dress . . . only look at me . . . I'm dying!"

Eliante, at present standing over the neck of the white amphora, became taut as a bow from head to foot. She was not offering herself to the man; she was giving herself to the alabaster vase, the one insentient person on the scene. Without a single indecent gesture, arms chastely crossed on this slender form, neither girl nor boy, she clenched her fingers a little, remaining silent, then, the man saw her closed eyelids flutter, her lips half open, and it seemed that starlight fell from the whites of her eyes, from the enamel of her teeth; a slight shudder traversed her body—or rather a squall lifted the mysterious wave of her dress—and she gave a small groan of imperceptible joy, the very breath of orgasm.

Either it was the supreme, the splendid manifestation of love, the god actually descending to the temple, or the spectator had in front of him the most extraordinary actress, an artist transcending the limits of possibility in art.

He was dazzled, delighted, indignant.

"It's scandalous! Right there . . . in front of me . . . without me? No, it's horrible!"

He threw himself on her, intoxicated by a mad fury.

"Actress! Horrible actress!"

She roused herself gently, very calm, smiling, her lips only a little paler under their artificial carmine.

"Leave me alone, then. . . . I am very content, you could add nothing better. Why are you making those ferocious animal eyes at me? Believe me, it's not because of virtue that I forbid you to touch my dress . . . it's because . . . it's over . . . I have given you what I can *show* a man of love."

Leon Reille was positively forgetting that he was wearing a suit, but she pulled away, and laughed openly.

"Ah! A man who doesn't know how to watch *love* is so silly. You really needed a lesson. Now, run along quickly. . . .

I can hear my coachman getting impatient in front of the gate."

And as he didn't move . . . she quickly pressed a bell.

A servant entered, half asleep:

"Tell Jean to drive the gentleman home, it's raining too hard for me to let him leave on foot."

Leon Reille was obliged to take his leave, in spite of himself.

"The curtain falls!" he thought.

CHAPTER TWO

"DEAR madam and . . . friend,

"Thank you for the very spiritual lesson you gave me, exactly one week ago, and I am writing to apologize for not having sent the customary bunch of flowers, or having attempted the pious digestive visit, but that exquisite lesson has led, for your humble servant, to such disagreable things that I judge it more necessary to become completely . . . the lowest of boors!

"Yes, dear madam, I feel so little enthusiasm for ancient vases in the form of a girl that I resolved, the very day after my expedition to the impossible, to cure myself of their burning memory by a little trip to the land of vulgar reality. (Please understand that I have thrown myself, prostrate, into the most dissolute debauchery!)

"I, madam, am playing, in the midst of the comedy of life, the role of the poor, austere boy, bothered because austere, barely going out except to hang around hospital rooms where he probes every human filth capable of smothering the ideal, which forces him to remain a very wretched materialist.

"I scarcely have the time to see a dream approach, before

I already have the urge . . . to rid my brain of it by every means debated by morality, but tolerated by the police.

"I live on the fifth floor, near the roof, and I have almost a nervous terror of hearing certain tomcats caterwauling, on cat carnival nights, the example, invisible though it may be, seems to me to be so contagious.

"However, I feel equally the nervous terror of evenings in the beer hall, not smoking a pipe, and Bullier dances,[1] not knowing how to dance at all as I think I already told you. (It was, goodness knows, a little for these various reasons that I sought to distract myself in salons where people chat, these being sometimes more hospitable than any other establishment and maintaining, despite the heavy closed curtains, an appearance of decency which sufficiently excites your sentimental side!)

"Alas! I returned, from these illustrious salons, sickened, ill, all sentimentality more than withered, attacked by an *exotic*—to put it politely—fever, and swearing I would never be caught there again . . . so far as one can ever swear! . . . At your home, madam and friend, I met a strange creature who acted out for me with the prettiest of style and gestures, a monstrous, well-known love story, tiring mainly for the spectators, entitled, in the sort of salons where people do not chat, *The Maid of Nanterre*. I dare to spell out this title to you in full because you will grasp its real beauty; however, it would be useless to ask for it at your bookstore. The good man might take you for an *ingénue* . . . or get angry. I have too much respect, madam, for your severe inconsolable widow's dress to tell you what happened between this strange creature and me during one terrible night of pouring rain. The next day, then, aching all over, very indignant at *exoticism*, I went for a walk in the various places one can meet consolable widows . . . no, plaster vases, carefully stuccoed, stamped, never crumbling during numerous washes and full of compliance, if not of rosy sentiment. I made the acquaintance of a charming . . . jug from Montmartre, blond, plump, white—she has precisely that appetising fold of marble that you had the goodness to bring to my attention—and she talks absolutely . . . like a jug! Let me be frank: she can scarcely utter a single word, always the same, one which will remind you no doubt of Tunisian caravans. She says: *Camel*,[2] and she says it ineffably (when she burns herself tasting soup!) What do you expect? *exoticism* has perverted my senses to the point that the little person from Montmartre seems to me to have fallen from Mohammed's paradise, a receptacle of pure form, a celestial amphora, the veritable chosen vessel! The first night after you know which, the *unforgettable* one, everything came off (if you will excuse the expression) prodigiously. In the morning, I found myself once again gay, well-disposed, light-headed and -hearted, the proof being that the mere appearance of one of your black, taloned gloves in my home would have had the same effect on me as a "Bless you" after a copious series of sneezes. The second night of debauchery, also spent analyzing the charms of my personal amphora (expensive, though hardly unique on the market), I began to feel a slight palpitation under my left breast. I rarely go in for heartache in society. I dread it greatly in the arms of a pretty girl, no, the handles of a pretty Parisian jug, and since I am in a bad mood when I feel these palpitations, I thought it best to get up and consult, in my shirt, my Dieulafoy.[3] Very salutory, the study of medicine, O madam, in these sad circumstances! It is surprising how much light is shed on the most obscure problems! The delicious child, woken by the untimely manifestation of my austerity, began suddenly to cry. (What better to do than overflow when one is a vase full . . . of candor?) She declared that in a dream I had uttered a name other than hers, a woman's name, and that I was deceiving her with one of her best friends whom she calls: *the Normandy Sole*. I tried in vain to explain to her that the sweet name of Eliante (so ridiculous between you and me), was not a woman's name, that it could at most be used to label one of the two chastity belts in the Cluny Museum; my personal jug didn't want to let it go. Alas! worldly vase or naive jug, it's amazing how subtle women are. *Normandy Sole*! *Eliante Solo*! It's all the same to them. I had to submit, then, to the flow of a torrent of insults, to hear myself called as many names as the caravan animal which transported, long ago, across the immensity of the desert, the most beautiful ornament in your salon, madam. And that made me really furious: I do not have the patience of those guardians of the harem where they unearth, to please your pretty eyes, the sacred carafe of love which satisfies your thirst. After letting all the camels go by me, I ended up flicking off the alabaster fold of my young friend of forty-eight hours, and she deigned to respond with a slap capable of bringing a dromedary to its knees. That hurt a lot. I kept the caravan but returned the slap. A regular set to, O madam and dear teacher! Broken furniture, my Dieulafoy torn, a large book which was very useful, and a petticoat of lace . . . (imitation Valenciennes) reduced to shreds! You'll admit that it's a lot of noise for just one name and which name? (That's a real 1830, that one!) I had to leave my personal jug; for it was impossible to pour anything into it except gold coins: so much for the real tears, so much for the imitation Valenciennes lace and so much for the flicks and scratches, having damaged the little tobacco jar of my dreams. I keep only the dromedaries as small comfort. It's not much.

"Here I am once again alone, austere, bothered because austere, splenetic, ready to haunt high society with a pale face, black eyes, a pronounced taste for *exoticism*, that is to say for rest after victory.

"Hum! Victory? . . . I most certainly don't want to brag! It's a paltry victory that is won . . . by *decanting*.

"I am not sending you flowers. (Do you like tuberoses?) And I will not pay a digestive call. (Which day can one find you at home without the niece of the innocent sleep, deaf brother-in-law or servant on a spring?) But . . . I do want to see you again.

"Besides, you know, I will break your colorless pot, I will knock it over, your hypocritical widow's funeral urn! Yes, yes, I will strangle that bottle neck stinking of alchemy! Do I have the right to ask for, to demand, the explanation of a Chinese juggling act? I do not love you, and it is very unlikely that I shall end up becoming jealous of a Tunisian jug, only, I swear to you that on Saturday, at around three o'clock, I am going to see if at your house there is any man besides a dotard or a valet.

"Answer me. I am waiting . . . "

Leon Reille

"Sir and dear lover,

"I am at home on Fridays."[4]

Eliante Donalger

"Sir and . . . dear lover!" murmured Leon Reille confused by the little frosted card. "This woman is mad! What if I didn't go?"

CHAPTER THREE

HE arrived at around five o'clock the following Friday, to be more proper, more part of *her world*, and he found, at her house, a surprisingly bourgeois salon. He had entered by a door other than the one in the little garden, it was obvious at once.[1] An ordinary house, green plants with ordinary appearances, ordinary curtains from the Louvre, a maid who retained her country accent, and, in this salon, on the second floor, nondescript people; an old man with white whiskers who resembled a casino diplomat, two very fat ladies, one of them haloed by a hat decorated with an owl, a young girl of twenty trying to pass for ten and dressed in a choirboy's smock, her braided hair thumping against her back, finally Madame Donalger. That is to say Eliante, visiting Madame Donalger.

He no longer recognized this woman at all. She was wearing a tailored suit, black, of course, but ordinary and stained by an awful violet tie with white polka dots. Her hair was done in a very fashionable little fluffy puff, and she had a yellow complexion, without makeup, the ivory complexion of a woman who is suffering . . . or who has had too much fun.

People chatted.

The old diplomat represented the deaf brother-in-law. He talked loudly, was not aware of anything that was going on, solemnly discussed the health of the President of the Republic with the woman with the owl halo. As for the girl, she was presented imposingly like a collection plate at church:

"Here, Monsieur Reille, this is my niece, Missie, who has a cold. Since you are a bit of a doctor, give her a sermon. She insists on wearing a low-cut dress to go to the theatre tonight. And it's not even a premiere! A second performance at the Odeon . . . in your neighborhood . . . "

He had to sit down on a *very hard* Récamier couch, with this somewhat boney young lady, a girl with big tibias, holding her elbows like pick handles, and beautiful with that overly facile diabolical beauty which seduces only the apoplectic.

"My dear aunt told me you were at the ball for *tubercular children*, sir? Was there dancing?"

And she looked at him furtively, her physiognomy suitably malevolent, her eyes shining, trying to stick the point of her burgeoning simpleton's wit into the bluish depths of the eyes of the passionate young man.

He grumbled:

"Of course not, mademoiselle, you can't dance when you cough, it's forbidden, and it would be an even greater imprudence for you to wear a low-cut dress . . . from what I've seen."

"So you've never seen my aunt dance, have you! She puts everything into it, once she gets going. It's true she dances . . . in a dress with a high collar."

If he had seen her dance? Oh! yes, and a whirlwind went by in a dream. A black waltzing woman whose skirts flew up like dark acanthus leaves around the beautiful forbidden fruit, with a smooth and supple body, which one imagined whiter, smoother and more supple because it was veiled in mourning. Mourning for whom? Mourning for what? A terrible mourning planned in advance, to arouse the interest of pierrots whose imagination, soured early on, had scratched around in Baudelaire's dungheap, on rainy days. Damn it all! . . .

So they talked of tuberculosis patients being completely cured without, for all that, the slightest reduction in cases of lung disease, and he spat out the phrases of a serious man who possesses a fixed judgement on every issue. Even if he was only twenty-two, he knew the different ways of being politely stupid.

Disheartened by his useless visit, Leon Reille turned to the niece to try and learn a little about this house.

Mademoiselle Marie Chamerot, known as *Missie*, the daughter of a dead sister of this Monsieur Donalger, the naval officer destined never to return, fortunately, was a tall person, taller than Eliante. She seemed endowed with perpetual motion, and she ingenuously broke the china saucers. Every second, she would stand up, pick up an object, a spoon, some sugar, a cup, move the furniture, and one would hear a shattering laugh, as sharp as verjuice, or shattering porcelain. She sneezed from time to time. She shivered with fever and cold under her choirboy's smock, and her braid, thumping against her back, a braid of light chestnut hair, gave her a comic animalness, since she was called *Missie*. She reminded one a bit of a thin, shivering greyhound with its tail between its legs. The worst of it is that she sat down at the piano, without having to be asked, and she sang, in spite of her cold, repeating that she was going to copy Yvette,[2] by sniffing at the end of each couplet. She emphasized all the smutty parts, and, returning to the Récamier couch from the piano, she lit a cigarette and crossed her legs:

"Do you smoke, dear sir? It's excellent for colds, you know."

Leon Reille was flabbergasted. He was well aware that the upbringing of the day tolerated these tomboyish mannerisms, but he imagined that such a huge she-devil of an idiot must get in the way terribly in Eliante's salon. Mademoiselle Missie did not seem bad-tempered, she stuck to crass looks at the most, and she could have become pretty, if she had understood how natural, or artificial, grace colors with illusion the body of a woman, young or old.

"No, I don't smoke . . . at least not in front of girls!" he replied phlegmatically.

He reflected too that the night with the Eliante of love had slipped by completely without him, a cigarette smoker, having regretted for an instant that he had not dared light a single one.

He looked at Eliante, the Eliante visiting Madame Donalger. Deep in a big armchair, completely black, completely hermetic, she neither smiled nor moved, her closed eyes outlined by a brush stroke on her white ivory face like the eyes of a doll. Her modish little hairstyle did not suit her, she was proper and Parisian in a dignified way, but she kept her eyes to herself and for the evenings when she went to paint the town red, when it is permissible to caterwaul certain things . . . hardly French. The only thing which could be seen to emerge from her bizarre, exciting and magical charm were the little feet like mouse snouts which she put on a Pompadour footstool, the color of rose cream.

"Your niece is charming!" ventured Leon, who had stood up during the hubbub of the piano and who came and positioned himself behind the big armchair.

"Isn't she," sighed Madame Donalger in all seriousness. "She's an excellent girl, very knowledgeable, she has diplomas, and she could, if necessary, translate your . . . Dieulafoy. If she enjoys playing the child, it's because she's convinced it suits her type of beauty better."

Leon Reille choked back a violent urge to laugh:

"Translate my Dieulafoy? You think, do you, that we learn everything in Latin . . . "

"I don't know, I don't know anything. . . . I don't want to know anything."

And she clenched her little mouse feet on the Pompadour footstool.[3]

"There is, however, one thing that I want you to know, Madame Eliante," he murmured very quietly, as some noisy chords were struck, for Mademoiselle Missie had just returned to Yvette's ballads. "*I will break the jug!*"

"I beg you, be quiet, sir. My brother-in-law is watching us."

"Bah! Since he's deaf."

Monsieur Donalger, the brother-in-law, exclaimed:

"Ah! the Latin Quarter, young man! My old Latin Quarter, it hasn't changed, I assure you."

Armed with an extremely rudimentary diplomacy, the good man could not imagine that a medical student, introduced for the first time, should talk of anything but his environment.

"Goodness! you weren't lying . . . " added Leon. "He really is deaf. . . . Like the famous virgin pot." (He continued, louder.) "No, the Latin Quarter will never change, it is still inhabited by ruffians and blockheads who still hum the same tunes, they hiss at or follow . . . women! Ah! what a good time, sir, is had in the old Latin Quarter!" And he disguised a yawn of very real fatigue.

"Bad subject!" the deaf man threw at him, with a special laugh, for he had applied himself well in his simple deductions.

The two ladies took their leave, recommending to Missie a new score of *Manon*, a deluxe edition which everyone should own because of its binding.

"It makes a very nice New Year's gift," declared the one with the owl halo.

"And it looks good on the corner of the piano," agreed the second, who paraded only a modest half a dove.

When the two women had left, Missie exclaimed, between two sneezes:

"What bores! they never say anything funny, and they're afraid of music-hall songs!"

Eliante added quietly, with a half-smile of complicity:

"It's because of their hats."

Leon smiled too, and the brother-in-law declared peremptorily:

" . . . But they were wrong to put through the Boulevard Saint-Michel, because it joins the two banks of the river, and people don't stay in their own place."

This time everyone began to laugh openly.

"A cup of tea?" asked Eliante, turning to the old man, with a sudden deference, as if she wanted to destroy the ridiculous effect, to indicate that she would allow one outburst of laughter, but no more.

"With pleasure, only I don't have my cakes. Missie forgot them, you know, my apricot cakes?"

Missie, with the gesture of a Bouillon Duval waitress,[4] said:

"Ah, what a fuss!"

She ran anyway to fetch the cakes in question, because Eliante, with a slight nod, had motioned to the door.

So, satisfied in smug anticipation, the old glutton curled up by the fireplace to poke a big piece of glowing wood.

"Yes, I shall break the jug, Madame Eliante," repeated Leon, sitting down beside her, on the same Récamier couch which seemed softer.

A transformation took place. Eliante opened her eyes. She was beautiful.

"Why do you want to hurt me?" she said, pulling back her dress with the sudden movement of a schoolgirl who is frightened . . . or having fun. "I haven't broken anything of yours, have I, sir."

"Ah! You haven't broken anything of mine? You have just ruined my life for a week, I went on a binge at exactly that point in the book where I was supposed to study, and I began reading at exactly that point where the most elementary prudence recommends on the contrary that you have a thoroughly good time. . . . Nothing broken! What about my furniture! And my Dieulafoy! and my personal amphora? You call that nothing, do you!" (He furtively slid his hand onto her knee, and squeezed it, passionately.) "And I have debased myself into the bargain, because it is debasing to give the name of the woman you want to the one you don't desire. Moreover, just from the hygienic point of view, it's deplorable. Eliante, why do you write letters beginning with that colossal sentence: *Sir and dear lover*! If you think I'm going to give it back to you! . . . Hum! You have really compromised yourself, madam. I'm going to show that, I assure you, to all my friends in the Latin Quarter. Don't worry, I don't have many. *Sir and dear lover? I am at home on Fridays!* Your letter may not be long, but the devil take me if I can make out what you mean. You aren't my mistress . . . "

She was playing with a little spoon, affectedly stirring a mixture of tea, rum and lemon.

"You thought of giving it back, then," she asked, half smiling, a little perfumed smile in which there was a lemon drop of banter.

"Here it is!" admitted the young man simply, and he held out to her the frosted card which had been burning his skin for two days above his heart.

"No, sir, I never take back what I give." (She exclaimed, slightly surprised.) "Oh! How hot it is, is that how hot you are inside your chest? No, no, keep my letter . . . or burn it, but I think you already have."

"All right, I'll keep it . . . like a marriage vow. You have seduced me, I am the gentleman victim. I am entitled to reparation."

"Certainly! Marry my niece, since you find her charming?"

"Oh! no, I don't like women whose arms and legs are like prison bars. Thank you very much. Besides, raised by you, she must have unusual ideas about *stock pots*."

"Raised by me, sir, she would have been, I am convinced, either a beautiful and decent wife, or a great and witty courtesan. But Monsieur Donalger sent her to school. She will only be a clever monkey, ignorant of the art of being a woman . . . you are perhaps wise not to marry her. You are too . . . young."

"And I assure you, dear Eliante, that I have no desire to get married, neither now nor later." (He pressed a little against her hip under the pretext of reaching the sugar bowl.) "Is it sugar you are looking for, madam?" he shouted very loudly, to provoke a response from the old diplomat.

"Pah!" said he, his head in the ashes. "Our town council put up magnificent monuments for them, but I don't think they're any more assiduous in their classes than in my time. Youth must take its course!"

"I absolutely agree with you," whispered Leon quietly. "And if Madame Eliante wishes to help me. . . . It will take its course exquisitely. Eliante, my letter, that I wrote, didn't offend you."

" . . . Amused, rather! You are somewhat brutal, and you certainly wrote to ruffle me. . . . Well . . . I've already answered you."

"Yes: *Sir and dear lover*! Are you still making fun of me?"

"I always tell the truth . . . in principle."

"So now I'm your lover . . . in theory?"

"If you like . . . "

"Yes, I like!"

They had reached this point in their feverish chat, quite mundane in appearance, when Missie arrived, carrying a tray of cakes.

"I couldn't find them! There's no one in the pantry, no one in the antechamber, and, if we're supposed to go to the theatre, I wonder how we're going to have dinner? I say, aunt dear, invite the gentleman! He can drive us, it's almost in his neighborhood." (She sneezed.) "As for me, I'm feeling better."

The kind of order which reigned throughout the girl's brain, spread itself throughout her speech. At the very moment she deplored the absence of the servants, she invited a new gentleman to dinner, without worrying about the opinion of her relatives present in the room, and she declared her cold to be cured while sneezing as loudly as the cymbals of a bass drum.

Cakes flew off the plate onto the carpet. Monsieur Donalger let out an exclamation of despair. Madame Donalger pinched her lips together, those lips which had just pronounced an *if you like*! that would damn a saint, and she coughed in a serious tone, seeking to catch *Missie's* eye.

"Now what's the matter!" said the young lady in her smock, blowing her nose, while Leon picked up the cakes to look virtuous. "Make eyes at me all you want? That won't get you *anywhere*; the gentleman is a student, and I shall be a lady doctor when it suits me, so we are *pals*! You say yourself that I pick up science like a sponge!"

Very proud of this new effect, she burst out laughing, the good-natured laugh of an obtuse boy.

Leon copied her. What a strange house and how well he would do to become intimate with these ladies! If this were the source of the *exotic* perfume, he would get used to it. This sort of big monkey disguised as a choirboy, with a husky voice, a manner not too vicious, only giddy, clumsy and hurried, riding on Paris life, her eyes fixed, her tongue sticking out, coming first in all her classes and doing somersaults in salons, like a circus clown (breaking conscientiously, moreover, china cups that deserved a better fate, these cups which Eliante alone seemed to know how to juggle), this big ape, moderately female, soon represented the foil to set off the rarity of the other, the window display model. The other need say nothing. This one, once she was wound up, would chatter for hours, strike chords, smash porcelain and would fidget and flap, fanning with her girlish skirts, her badly plaited braid, the mysterious idol who was refreshed by the youth scattered around her as one is refreshed by the breeze of green palms.

It was necessary to really press Leon Reille. He was dreading the second supper, so different, no doubt, from the first he had been served downstairs, on the garden side. On the courtyard side . . . , it would perhaps be boring. Then he thought about the numerous boxes of candy, the bunches of flowers he would have to pile up on the tables of this salon to equalize the situations, the chances.

"No, really, I can't," he murmured, vexed. "It would be too indiscreet," (and he emphasized the phrase) "too indiscreet . . . the same day as I pay a visit . . . formally."

Eliante smiled:

"You'll come back next Friday, that's all there is to it."

He took a deep breath, let himself slide. . . . It was warm in this salon, both exotic and bourgeois at once. There, one breathed an atmosphere of sweet intoxication. The brother-in-law with his rheumatism never took his ailments further than the Trocadéro and gave up accompanying his nice relatives in society, for he really was too deaf to be a former Embassy attaché who had had the ear of ministers.

The dinner was hardly complicated. On the first floor,

Missie took care of the interior, that much could be guessed from the way the maid, while stubborn, obeyed, the way the table was set and the fruit was on the dish.

During this dinner, Leon Reille learned that Madame Donalger was a French creole, born of parents so French they had perished in the 1870 war: the father of a saber cut, the mother of sorrow.[5] She had been placed in a boarding school, and she left only to get married, to Monsieur Donalger, the younger brother of the diplomat, a naval officer.

During one of Missie's absences, when she went to fetch a flask of island liqueur, scolding the maid the length of the corridor, the young man, able to bear it no longer, asked a burning question:

"Did you love him, this husband?"

She lowered her head a little.

"He was forty years old, I was seventeen.[6] I came out of a convent, out of a sad house to enter a sad house: a big black vessel rolling across the most dangerous oceans. I saw and heard terrible things in that ship! The window of my bedroom, a magnificent nest of fabrics and furs, didn't even have fifty centimeters' view of the sea. I never breathed comfortably there, and when I set foot on land, the sun hurt me, I would hear guttural accents which terrified me. Back in France, it was official receptions all the time, solemn dinners . . . and we set off again without knowing where for. When my husband died, it seemed to me that the convent wall was crumbling . . . but on me . . . since he had a very poor family: his brother, Missie: I was rich, I owed him my entire fortune and, not having any children, I had to take in my relatives, still live . . . as a prisoner. . . . The family, you see, is daily semi-mourning! Hush! Don't answer. Missie has just returned."

Leon Reille listened to her in a spin. She froze him, now, with her gloomy, slightly singsong voice of a capricious creole who is always cold, a bird of paradise with feathers painted for other skies. She wasn't born to look after children or care for old men, that was obvious.

"Are you cold at home?" he murmured while Missie poured the liqueur separately, far from them, into mauve glasses.[7]

"Yes."

"Is that why you dare not show more of yourself?"

"No! I have leprosy," she answered calmly.

"You're going to make me believe that? I beg you, don't repeat it, I'm starting to shiver too, myself. What a woman! I'm going to hate you!"

"That's because we don't *yet* speak the same language? That will come!"

Missie served the little glasses of liqueur and paraded them one by one, like amethysts on a necklace.

"There!" cried the diplomat holding up a delightful chalice after having devoutly warmed it in his hands. "One would think it was flower blossom, blossom made flesh. Try that, young man, our dear Eliante makes this mixture with her ball bouquets. An excellent violet cream, much better than what they sell in English establishments."[8]

"The nuns taught me that recipe, and they made a big fuss about it, like a confessional secret," said Eliante simply.

"As for me," declared Missie sneezing, "I think it burns the chest, you have to be my aunt to swallow that . . . or my uncle! Goodness gracious! I'm having some because I want to go out this evening, but what a fire. You'd think it had all the fires of hell in it, your nun's cream."

"Good lord!" breathed Leon, annoyed. "A recipe found in the bottom of the Tunisian vase."

For all that he spoke softly, Missie heard and raised her eyes, her eyes which wept from her cold and the liqueur.

"What, you know about the white vase, do you?"

"Yes, no; that is to say, mademoiselle, that madam your aunt has told me a little about it . . . at the tubercular children's ball."

"Well, even I, as I stand before you," (and the girl tapped herself on the chest), "I have never glimpsed it. My aunt doesn't want me going into her rooms."

"Come, come, mademoiselle, I think you are too reasonable to . . . have the good idea of destroying the slightest pot of that type!"

"Goodness, my dear child," replied Eliante getting up to finish the meal, decisively, "I asked you not to come down to my rooms because, in them, there are some objects, souvenirs of my husband, which are fragile. I wouldn't scold you if you wanted to have some respect for them instead of trying to see them."

"Oh! my dear aunt, I'm certain that would bore me to tears. . . ." (She turned to Leon.) "Just imagine, there are enough little men to fill a small room, little Chinese gods doing strange things and also crocodiles, snakes, spiders, heaps of fantastic animals . . . then she also has crates full of robes, extraordinary, beautiful robes. Naturally, none of that is appropriate for a girl. I wanted, one fine morning, to get to the bottom of it, and I went on tip toe. . . . My aunt was sleeping . . . She sleeps until noon. I examined everything, except the white vase, which she hadn't yet bought, at that time, I came back feeling pretty silly! If that's all that's forbidden to girls . . . I didn't understand any of it, and it didn't seem much fun to me. . . . She can rest easy . . . I won't go down there again, even for the Tunisian pot."

"You should always listen to your aunt!" scolded the old diplomat mechanically, in complete digestive beatitude and with the tender respect that ruined old men have for rich young women.

Missie burst out:

"But I do listen! . . . since I'm telling you it bores me to tears. But I'm not blind. I know where children come from, they taught me in school."

Leon Reille felt like he had just received a lash of the whip on one side and a cold shower on the other.

"My sincere compliments, mademoiselle, as for me, I admit I don't know it yet for certain, although I'm a future doctor."

"Missie, Missie!" repeated Madame Donalger, scandalized. "The gentleman doesn't know you well enough for you to make such . . . knowledgeable confessions. . . . Go and get dressed, why don't you, and above all cover up well."

"No, I'm going to wear bare skin. . . . Back in a little while, sir."

Then, with a sudden movement, knocking her chair over backwards, she ran and threw herself on Eliante, who was about to go downstairs.

"My dear aunt . . . oh my dear, dear aunt . . . I love you so much! I adore you, even . . . kiss me, you aren't angry . . . what's more you're so good, my beautiful dear aunt!"

Standing, nervously, in front of the two women as they kissed, the young man felt like asking for his share. Fortunately, the old diplomat slipped a box of Havana cigars under his nose.

"Ah," said Monsieur Donalger clicking his tongue. "Isn't she amusing, my little niece? She is the joy of our household."

One hour later the two women reappeared all dressed up. Eliante in a dress of spangled black tulle with a satin background, and Missie wearing a violent blue with tufts of daisies, nevertheless a bit babyish for her robust twenty years. To erase the marks of her head cold, she had borrowed her aunt's rice powder and had smeared it on with touching care, putting it everywhere except where it was needed. One eye and her nose were still streaming, she displayed hollow collar bones, elbows with points like nutcrackers, and plebeian, badly cared-for hands, since they wouldn't fit into Madame Donalger's old gloves, which she insisted on preferring to her own new ones, because they were more *stunning*, from the best store, and she had put her hair up in a loose bun to copy Eliante, who, for her part, had gone back to her original hairstyle, the bonnet of smooth hair, stuck to the temples and setting off her superb eyes like a velvet brim overhanging two jewels. Simply but carefully made-up, slimmed by a sheath dress like a torrent of ink, Eliante had the appearance of a black siren, agile on her sinuous tail, as though more free without feet.

For one minute, Leon and she found themselves together at the bottom of the stairs, Missie having forgotten her fan.

"The young lady your niece seems to love you tenderly?" said the young man gnawing the edge of his hat.

"Oh! she's a good girl, not at all fanciful, only sometimes she weighs heavily on me, the dear! She is noisy, untidy, much too modern for my feeble lazy nature, and I'm afraid I won't see her married before . . . "

"Before you?" interrupted Leon very disturbed.

"Me? I don't want to remarry, my dear child, I have passed the age . . . I have to remain free. I insist on running around at whatever time I choose, going out alone, getting away frequently from where I live, because I'm a little wild, I have to seek adventure according to my capricious nature of a beast brought up on all fours.[9] Creoles, sir, are not put in diapers and strapped up in *swaddling clothes*, they are left naked wandering on the ground in the very first days of their infancy. A custom of the land. These days, I close myself up in extremely high-necked dresses in order to earn a compensation. Since people realize that I am not a coquette, I can go very far . . . "

"Indeed, dear madam, right up to allowing certain suppositions . . . "

"No . . . don't suppose anything, I don't want a husband any more, because it's too cumbersome, and I don't want a lover because. . . . I have the cure of souls here."

"You prefer pots?"

"You are very naughty, Leon my dear friend."

"Ah! so it becomes *sir and dear . . . friend* this evening?"

Missie came clattering down with her fan.

They got into the carriage, Leon on the small front seat, the two women at the back of the coupé. He was pressed between their knees barely clothed in light silks.

He ventured a few comparisons.

Missie's were pointed, as unyielding as sword handles, but she did not press them against him, on the contrary, she drew them back, a little afraid.

Madame Donalger let them be enveloped, possessed, without a scowl, a frown, to indicate that she suspected or deigned to suspect a thing.

He bent down to hunt again for the fan of that lunatic Missie, who dropped everything she held.

So he had the rude indecency to stroke Eliante's ankle beneath her skirt, and he climbed rapidly into the lace, encountering only the irritating coldness of the silk stocking, a reptilian coldness, then the smooth little apple of the well-rounded knee, finally the supple bracelet of the garter, where he stopped for a second to detail, with his fingernail, a complicated knot of ribbon and to injure himself on the hidden hook of a fastening.

Eliante, still immobile, murmured:

"Do you know what the play is this evening?"

He removed his feverish fingers, hesitated, and, seized with a senseless fury, he pinched her full on the skin, pinched her without restraint, wanting bitterly to see her struggle, give herself away, to hear her cry out, to make her spurt, a woman and all warm, exasperated, from her siren's wrapping.

In a very calm voice, she added:

"A drama or a comedy, dear sir?"

Missie, bad-tempered, blew her nose desperately.

"It's all the same to me! I'm going to have a red nose."

"I believe," breathed Leon, "that it's a comedy that . . . will become a drama towards the end!"

CHAPTER FOUR

"BUT of course, sir and dear lover, I want to write to you, only, *I don't know*, and it embarrasses me always to say what I think in a definitive manner. If I had a great deal of wit, I would amuse you at least, you who want so much to be amused.

"No, I haven't the wit, I will perhaps never have the wit to amuse you *according to your desires*. You said, no doubt, as you left us: *Farewell* for my niece Missie. I think she is like you, and one cannot see clearly the people who resemble one, at first; later, you get used to it and you no longer think to reproach them with holding up a mirror to you. She works very hard, and she is in a big hurry to have a good time, like you; so she has a bad time, she cries often, she's annoyed because she wastes time writing papers, reading big boring books, learning in what hygienic way and for the betterment of humanity one must make babies: she knows everything, except . . . *how to look as though she doesn't*! She is a very good girl. If you knew her better, you would certainly value her enough to ask us for her hand in marriage, and even if you were not to love her with a superhuman love, you would retain a natural affection for her, one of those solid affections on which one founds a family and one conceives, dividing one's heart into as many pieces as one has children, the art of going without what one doesn't have, which is to say *everything*. I am talking to you about Missie, but I'm not at all jealous. What can she take from me? I love you and I'm happy to love you. By marrying her, you would give me the certainty of an eternity of happiness, simply. You are just arriving, I'm leaving, there is thirteen years' difference between us, that is to say I possess a secret that you will penetrate only when I am dead, completely old; it would be my greatest triumph to hear you exclaim one evening, as you contemplate my white hair, my deep wrinkles, my dim eyes: "How right you were, Eliante!" For the greatest happiness of women is to be right one day, one hour, one second after being wrong all their lives . . . apparently.

"I love you very much, sir and dear Leon, because I have resolved to love you. You know my existence. I am a free recluse, a sort of emancipated nun, a lay priestess. I want only to convert you to my religion, which is the only one. If you hadn't come, I would not have thought to go looking for you, but I understood, when I saw you cross my path like a poor hounded wild animal, that you were destined for me. So I dare to grab hold of you. I call you my lover, and I have no desire to withdraw from you the proof of this complete gift of my person, because I want you to know once and for all, that I don't mean ordinary passion. Other women are very afraid to admit the gift of their person, and with reason, *since they are admitting a state of inability to conceive love*. When I become your mistress in the physical sense of the word, I shall hide myself, I shall be troubled, mainly in front of you, and I shall belong to you only if I want to stop loving you, or get rid of the importunity of your body standing between you and me. Meanwhile I find it pleasant to have you for my master without dreaming for all the world, really, of debasing you by making myself your mistress. As you have had the courage to declare to me: there is no shortage of girls in the form of alabaster jugs in the Latin Quarter . . . and one must drink when one is thirsty.

"You will not drink at my house. I am the sealed fountain of which the Scriptures speak, sir.

"A flirt? No! Depraved? I don't know . . . . Coquettish? . . . . I'm above all indifferent to worldly successes of that sort, my dear friend, and soul-searching conversations on either side of a Parisian fireplace leave me disgusted with every kind of conversation. . . . I know too well the things that make men turn pale, young or old, to need to blush behind a fan when I feel the approach of desire in black clothes.

"I prefer it completely naked.

"And it's because you have shown it to me almost completely naked that I am sure it's the messenger of Eros! You came on behalf of the god. Enter in, then, and abandon all hope of anything besides *love*. I'll allow you even to say out loud: 'I know her, she has a mark on her right hip!' What does it matter, since you'll never know for sure! I alone shall know that, face to face with my shadow, you dare not distinguish it from the rest of the night . . .

"You are sad and you are trying to appear jovial, crude, repeating phrases from fashionable romance. You are struggling against the need, the thirst for the supernatural that you have, and you don't believe in it, the great supernatural, you don't believe in it, you would be so happy to believe in it! You pinched my leg like a shop-assistant at the Louvre would have pinched my little finger in smoothing on a pair of new gloves, it's the base pleasure of humiliating the grand lady of love passing by chance on the market of love, I couldn't cry out in front of a girl (Missie is a virgin), and I didn't want to give you the false joy of my painful emotion, *I was out*. When I'm not receiving guests, I don't need to say that I'm at home. Now, I have a bruise above my garter. Yesterday, it was black, today it's blue, tomorrow it will be yellow . . . then it will go away. . . . It's merely an *erosion* . . . from an employee of Eros!

"You should be Eros himself, sir.

"You're not afraid of much if the story of the oriental vase, which is a legend, exasperates you. I don't only love an oriental vase, I love you too; you are handsome because no one, I do believe, has yet seen you. You have over your eyes a blue veil, of the same blue as the bruise you gave me above the garter: that is the curtain of the temple. Happy, my dear friend, she who draws it aside to read in you! You are not taller than my dear objet d'art, standing next to each other, you could be two very white brothers. Only my alabaster vase seems more harmonious to me, less savage in its attitude, immobilized in the loveliest human position, the sexless position.

. . . No, don't make those eyes at me, with the bluish veil drawn aside! I know what you're thinking. When I say: *sexless*, that doesn't mean I want to castrate anyone. My Tunisian urn is by turns a 'he' or a 'she,' for that's the way it likes it. She isn't forced to give an opinion, to prolong her satisfaction at feeling me caress her or to split with joy when I contemplate her. She is chaste, and I leave her chaste. You, I would like you to be a man.

"Go and see the wenches, my friend! Go and see the wenches!

"Now, let's talk more seriously.

"You are twenty-two years old, you are an orphan, and you will be a doctor of medicine soon. Instead of wasting your body in dangerous exercises, do you want to get married idiotically, but with intelligence?

"I'm not like those old mistresses who give their daughter to a lover who has cooled off. I'm more direct than that in matters! I'm proposing to you the only shameful bargain worthy of our mutual pride. Missie, Marie Chamerot, is really an honest child, having studied useless questions, but a good and docile instrument of maternity, if not to conceive love. She will become pretty if you want it. With a little love flesh on top of her virgin's flesh, she will round out her angles and take on more gracious looks. She isn't stupid, nor cruel, oh! no, she finishes off the little cats she steps on, so as not to see them suffer; she is incapable of any perceived bad action. She can become a very amusing companion merely by the alternation of her unconscious consciences. What's more, she speaks two languages properly: English and Italian, and she knows even better enough Parisian slang to distract a man's revery. Her hair is heavy. Her brain is heavy, but she must be taught to style her mind. She expects everything from a husband and has prepared nothing for him. I think I have explained my phrase: "I tried to make her a beautiful and witty courtesan." I must have scandalized you in telling you all this. I believe only in love, and I try to relate all my acts and all my words to it. She has understood nothing, if not that her very real honesty was moved to the point of turning for a moment towards ridiculous manifestations. She nearly *loved* me because . . . they will always love me who see me preach in the temple. I closed the sanctuary before the irreparable; if she hadn't remained an ignorant virgin, she would have fallen into a terrible bestiality, and no man would ever have been able to bring her out of the mire. I talked to her about religion as a mystic, she responded as . . . a medical student and that did not suit my truly amorous temperament. She would have wanted to help me, unconsciously, me the chosen one, to receive my god. . . . I don't need her. My god doesn't like girls like that, he needs priestesses who have seen no one but him. . . . As for me, I have no idea how to skim through books on modern medicine, I have skimmed through men. . . . I repeat: Missie is innocent, she spends her time making herself old through study and young through an affected childishness, which ages her even more. She has a small disappointment: a gentleman, absolutely ordinary, having obtained permission to court her, ended up asking me to marry him. She didn't love him, but, the day I threw the man out of the house, she cried. From that fateful day when a virgin glimpsed that love is perhaps a science one must know above all other sciences, and that it's not enough to be young to please, she has become an actress, awkwardly, alas! she *copies me*. And she has become, a terrible thing for a young girl, the caricature of an old woman. Now, she is no more jealous of me than I can be jealous of her, but she trembles, quite naturally, to think that she will lose everything . . . that I will always get everything before her.

"I wouldn't be the great criminal I am if I weren't absolutely loyal. I propose then that you marry Missie. I will give her, whatever happens, a very appropriate dowry, and she will be my beneficiary if she marries you. A serious doctor (you will surely become a serious doctor) is not obligated to his wife when she brings him a fortune. The man who works seriously, in a couple, even if he didn't earn a cent, is always the protector of his companion and owes her nothing.

"Don't imagine I'm setting a trap for you or that I want to put you to the test. It's more serious.

"If you please me, I want to preserve you like the Tunisian vase, and I have to put you in the shadows of happiness. Happiness is me, and Missie is the curtain. She will screen you . . . from my light! besides, you can easily refuse my offer, only, watch out! Don't try, later on, to obtain through personal intrigues what you have been offered wholeheartedly and loyally, reasonably. I don't forgive tricks that are vulgar.

"Next, don't think that I'm trying to marry off the girl with a stain.

"I want to keep you as long as possible, that's all, and give some happiness back to the one who can reproach me with being *myself*.

"Now, just as I had to use intermediaries to obtain an alabaster vase with a rare expression of form, I am obliged to . . . act as go-between to give you the chance to stay close to me, to both be happy through me.

"And I want to settle the deal *before* any other kind of transaction. Generally, women with experience don't have such lucidity, pronounced *loyalty*, in matters of love.

"Think about it! Bills of exchange of this kind should be signed in our blood. I warned you I didn't know how to write, but I know how to sign. I'm not being funny, I'm saying what is, what I think, everything I want. But you are free to not come back.

"I'll expect you on Sunday, around noon, at my rooms, come via the garden. We'll have lunch together.

"Depending on your answer, *I remain your servant for life*, and this phrase is not banal coming from my pen, o my little love friend."

Eliante Donalger

(By return post)

"No! I'm splitting my sides! . . . One would think them the revelations of a clairvoyant:

"'You will be a serious doctor . . . you will be the husband of an ugly young person, but rich . . . you will be . . .

"I'll be your lover and that's all there is to it, eh! or I'll teach you what stuff women like you are made of! If I had beaten you that night of our big sport, in front of the pot, you would love me without so much fuss!"

Leon Reille

(The same day, express letter)

"I offer my apologies for a rather short letter, sent this morning, which will reach you, I hope, after this one. I told you that you sounded like a clairvoyant. It's not quite right. Those women are sometimes poor devils who lure the naive, because they need to make a living. You! It's better or worse. You try to corrupt the imagination for nothing, simply to defile or . . . to amuse yourself even more, with the little hussy who is looking over your shoulder at this very minute, *my future fiancée*! I'll enter your house neither by door nor by window, I'll not write to you any more. I don't like actresses, procurers even less.

"I need more direct relations. I was ashamed of myself, having to satisfy my hunger for you with a wench. Now, I've lost my appetite. Your servant."

(Same day, telegram)

"Yes, Sunday at noon. As arranged."

L.R.

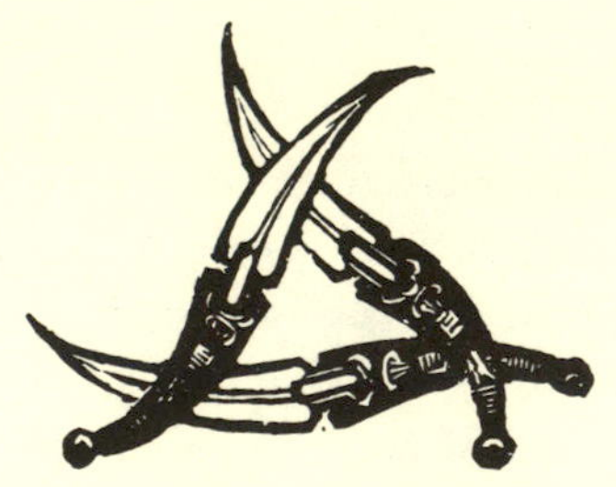

CHAPTER FIVE

LEON Reille, pushing open the little garden gate, felt his resolve weaken.

It was a fine winter day, a Christmas day. All over the immense town, bells could be heard ringing, mad bells which beat the air with their sonorous wings like robust birds. And it was the whole earth, this poor little garden full of mysterious shadow, this poor frozen earth, flowering with frost after having flowered basketfuls of rare beauty. But the sun shone on the frost, the bells hummed in an atmosphere of hope, they beat joyfully on the man's brain making his reason take flight, scattering it to the four corners of the earth. Christmas! Christmas! . . . Just when one hopes no more, one hopes still.

Leon had bought, for this holiday, a very elegant overcoat and a hat *without a spring*, a more fashionable hat. He did not want to appear a beggar for love, but *the master*, the one who would talk very loudly.

"After all, what am I doing here?" he mused, while his nervous step made the gravel crunch and he resolutely climbed the three steps to the entrance.

He lifted his head, caught sight of Eliante, standing,

her hands outstretched, in the green dining room, that room of silvery willow green where he had already dined one night. Eliante came forward to meet him, as white as an angel, she came toward him hospitably, as a maternal woman who knows perfectly well why her love friend has come on this holy day of Christmas, while the bells of deliverance ring madly, the robust bells of human folly! And, behind her, a good fire blazed, the table was set.

"Madam," he said, in a very cold tone he had *been preparing* since the doorstep, "I won't offer you my homage, I've come to get angry, so I think it's pointless to cover you with reproaches." (He added, shuddering a little): "Heavens! you're wearing white? It's strange. I thought you were an inconsolable widow? My compliments, moreover, white suits you very well."

Eliante was wearing a long dressing-gown of ivory velvet, decorated with reddish lace, her ballroom hairstyle, the bonnet of smooth hair twisted into a low helmet, topped by a large coral pin of curious workmanship. Without much makeup, Eliante's complexion seemed even whiter from the reflections of old ivory she wore around her, and her impeccable bust stood out clearly, without a fold, under the velvet of the bodice draped seamlessly.

"I believe a child is born to us this night, isn't it," she said, laughing a calm laugh, "for neither one of us has the look of people who have stayed up all night."

"You are mistaken, madam," replied Leon, in his same ceremonious tone. "On the contrary I have just come from a night of prolonged debauchery, which led me to find myself in the street at this hour and in your neighborhood. What child are we talking about?"

She closed the door, let fall the green silken folds which screened such a tender day the color of spring water.

Leon threw his hat and his overcoat onto a chair, with a gesture of rage.

"I meant that we have both conceived tonight, perhaps without knowing it, you amidst a student revelry, I dreaming in my bed, a god other than the one mortals are ordinarily concerned with. Now, don't answer right away. It's disastrous to get angry on an empty stomach! Sit down there, in front of the fire which is not too hot, I assure you, warm yourself up and let me serve you, we shall be free, in spite of all the servile attitudes it may suit us to take, for we are quite alone, at this moment, in the world. Missie has gone to the inauguration of a public nursery, and my brother-in-law is accompanying her. As for me, I was expecting you."

"This really is the limit," grumbled Leon, removing his gloves from his feverish hands. "You were expecting me, dear madam? You might well have received a last telegram without flowers. At this student revelry, there was no shortage of women, I assure you!"

"Oh!" exclaimed Madame Donalger gaily, "four telegrams, including one letter, to confirm your single visit, would have been a lot, my dear friend, since you would have arrived on time anyway. As for the flowers, thank you. I just happen to have on my mantelpiece some superb Christmas roses which one of your friends, carousing with you probably, Monsieur Leon Reille, sent me around midnight . . . "

Leon Reille bit his lips. Since he had no mustache, one could easily pick out the smile rising in the cruelty of the bite. Yet, he suffered, his eyes showed glimmers of a storm, he clenched his naked hands.

"I've come. . . . I must explain . . . I don't want anything to eat, you understand! Madam, you really must take me for a pot for sale? . . . Eliante! Tell me, aren't you ashamed?"

She remained calm, graciously worldly:

"I'm not at all ashamed to love, better than the vain grimaces of a vulgar love, a man who dares . . . without worrying about the possible consequences. You didn't know me when you followed me through the streets of my obscure neighborhood before following me through ballrooms? And you sought me discreetly, keenly, as one seeks supreme joy. You didn't know me when you said to a girl who had to disappear under the power of words, that . . . you preferred me. Faith begins thus . . . one follows blindly, and one finds. . . . Dear Leon of love, you will marry my niece."

She burst out laughing.

"No, I'll marry nothing at all! Give me something to drink, I'm choking! And I'm afraid to insult you too loudly! come on, Eliante! I reread your letter carefully before coming. What is this new comedy, and what symbol, black or white, is she hiding?"

"No symbol, I neither can nor do I want to marry you, so I'm offering you eternity in another form . . . since you're always mixing people up . . . "

"Let's not joke any more! Do you love me, do you, Eliante? Do-you-love-me?"

He put his elbows on the set table and stared at her, forcing himself to stay calm.

Surrounded by the nuptial enchantment of her robe, she seemed very young, and her arms could be seen in the wide sleeves of the gown, her arms whiter against the lining of yellow silk. They were small like those of a child, neither thin, nor chubby, only small, giving rise to a feeling of childishness, and her small powerful hands ran, like separate individuals, carrying skirts trimmed with lace, rummaging around objects, creatures always in a state of agitation. Leon's pupils gradually dilated as he watched her hands dancing, so timidly, always fleeing, and the cruel irony of his mouth melted,[1] in the end, into a real smile of hope.

"Eliante, look at me, instead of uncorking that bottle? No, your poisons will inebriate me no longer; I really thought about it last night. You must belong to me first . . . we'll talk afterwards. Those are my conditions. As for the rest, I don't care."

She poured some amber wine for him in his glass and chose some water for herself.

"Don't hurt me needlessly," she said, removing her hand from his. "We aren't in the carriage now! Yes, I'm looking at you, yes, you are a very attractive boy, with a serious mask, pure features, you don't make faces easily, with eyes veiled as though they are about to cry, and you never cry, do you, you are too proud? My ambition would be to see you cry with love . . . "

She withstood the blow of his fixed pupils without any apparent embarrassment and seemed to be staring at something inside him, something other than himself.

"I'm tired," he said in a very low voice, his eyelids suddenly closed, "I don't want to die of sorrow, but I'm sleepy, you don't scare me, since you still attract me, you just humiliate me, Eliante, I have nothing to give you but myself, take me and don't keep on giving me charity. I'm really suffering, they are much too long, these preambles, I never cry, as you say . . . you won't have that pleasure. I can't understand how a woman can stay like this with no sign of physical emotion in front of a man who wants her. . . . You are horrible, if not ridiculous."

When he opened his eyes, Eliante was on her knees before him and the train of her white skirt burned with all the reflections of the fire like a huge opal. She really was on both knees, her two small hands joined.

"I want," she said, in a very soft voice whose softness contrasted with the violence of her words, "I want you to know what I know, for you to go as far as me, I demand and I have the right to demand that you choose me as I choose you. You must *learn* about me before you *earn* me! and if you are already tired, you must allow me to *want* it in your place!"

Leon bent over her.

"Give me your mouth, at least?"

"You won't know how to kiss me. I'm afraid, I am, of useless gestures. They are what spoil everything."

"Are you ill? Do you have some kind of infirmity? . . . I tell you I'm ready to overlook everything. I need you. I won't rest until I have you. . . ." (As she turned her head away, he stood her up on her train, taking her by the waist.) "I can only translate your resistance, Eliante, into a desire to be raped. Frankly, I no longer dare to resort to it. It's not my way. I sense in you an instrument of perdition, and those whom you have held in the tiny pincers of your eyelashes must have had a nasty moment . . . *before*. But, *after* . . . it must be very funny. . . . Answer me? Do you want to be raped? Killed? I wouldn't feel sorry for you!"

Eliante smiled.

"I'm already dead."

"Why?"

"I'll explain in a minute. Let's have lunch first, please, what do you say? I was so happy to feel you near me and you are distancing yourself . . . "

"All right, let's have lunch . . . let's talk about the weather, this and that . . . let's talk about everything except love, then!"

They sat down, one on either side.

Eliante uncovered a silver bowl in which eggs trembled on a fragrant purée.

"Do you like that, my dear friend? They are fresh eggs."

"So I see," said Leon with a shrug, "innocent fresh eggs, mother hen's eggs on a purée of my boiled brains, because I'm beginning to go mad . . . yes, I like that; to devour oneself, for want of something better, is a pastime."

She offered him the precious little saltshakers.

"Saffron or cumin?"

"Plain!" he said brusquely, twisting his napkin.

They ate.

"Leon," she asked, in her affectionate voice, "who are you? I don't really know you. I just *meet* you."

"I'm not anyone. If it suits you, however, to know that I represent the son of a worthy, provincial notary, I admit it? My parents are egoists who make sure that my memory doesn't disturb them. They live in Dôle, an ancient, paralysed town. Madame Reille, my mother, is a devout woman, silent, with no tenderness for the children who play on the avenue in front of her window. Monsieur Reille, my father, must somehow get his fun with the maids, when he finds any to hand. These people are indifferent to me. I write to them to let them know of my progress in the art of killing softly, and I'm already an old student. When I'm a doctor, next year, or the year after, they will stop sending me my modest allowance. They have only one son, but he is their enemy, the enemy of their purse. They are misers! When I think about them, which happens to me in my bad dreams, I'm afraid of them. Avarice is a closed door, you don't know what's happening behind it, and before knocking you feel anxious."

"Will you return to the provinces when you are a doctor?"

"No. I'll try to live here, or I'll go to the colonies and study the plague to . . . console myself."

"The colonies! A warm island . . . lots of flowers and the sea purring around you. Palm trees, big palm trees, and permission to run naked on the sand. Leon, that's my dream, my own dream, to go and live in the colonies!"

"You are free, Eliante."

"I have to marry my niece, bury my brother-in-law. . . . One is free only by killing everyone else . . . "

"Let's run away, the two of us."

"You would marry me in spite of . . . the thirteen years' difference?"

"I think so . . . but not in spite of the fortune. It's your situation which makes me the younger."

"You're right."

As he smiled, she added:

"You see, we get along marvelously, my little love friend."

He frowned:

"Let's not talk about love, or I'll get angry."

She prepared for him, in a little crystal dish, some frangipani tartlets she made herself. She took little boats of flaky pastry and put in them a yellow, unctuous cream which smelled more like the perfume you put on handkerchiefs than pastry, then she sprinkled the whole thing with vanilla.

"It's vile and pretty, what you're doing, madam!"

"But it's deliciously good, dear sir. Taste!"

She held out a tartlet, which he bit right up to her fingers.

"Why, it smells like soap," he declared, bad tempered.

"Do you want some more?"

"No thank you."

"Now we'll go and drink our coffee in my room."

"In front of the big Tunisian sugar bowl? An excellent idea, dear madam."

"No, in my bedroom. You don't know where I sleep . . . when I sleep; and I want to do you the honor . . . since you are my lover."

Leon Reille felt a thrill. However, he was beginning to get used to the unusual language of this creature, so ardent and so glacial.

Ironically, he offered her his arm.

"You overwhelm me, my dear . . . mistress!"

The young man no longer thought about raping her. Sulking for the sake of form, almost gay inside, he resolved to maintain all possible decorum. It was indeed a unique adventure. His simple student life wouldn't offer many like this. He found himself in the delicious situation of a man who isn't looking to drink any more because he is already a little intoxicated, but not enough to no longer dare to drink. He would wait for the chance. This woman's wit, spicy like a liqueur from the warm islands about which she had dreamed aloud, amused him enormously. He had overcome one barrier, leaving behind the costume of a conventional lover, that banal gallantry which forces the man to assume a panting appearance, slightly ridiculous when he is resisted in the name of an equally conventional virtue. She accorded him every right . . . except the right to exercise them. He remained the master, the expected, the dominator. She knelt before him, proffering magical words, exuding the powerful and troubling perfume of an incantation, and, despite her servile attitude, she remained, indeed, quite *the mistress*, the one who teaches love.

They turned to the opposite side of the old rose salon, where, mysteriously ghostly, the white vase reigned, the memory of which still humiliated Leon. Eliante opened a door under another curtain the color of green water.

"Ever since the death of my husband," she said in a restrained voice, "no man has entered here, not even my brother-in-law."

He didn't believe a word of it and teased:

"Flatterer! . . . In any case, since you don't take me for a man."

This bedroom, vast and dark, looked like a temple. The windows overlooking the garden were three in number, yellow and oval like precious stones, topaz jewels cut with large facets like window panes; they let in no daylight, only sunshine, whether there was any outside or not, a sort of murky sunlight mixed with smoke from a fire. On the walls hung long animal skins, framed by light bands of gold cloth, a thick material half silk, half metal, which threw sharp beams of light on the furs and gave them a fiery reflected lustre. Lions and panthers, brown bears and black, alternated, each one presenting its head in the center of a panel, quite dead heads with eyes shut, mouths closed, not losing their natural expression by showing the horrible artificial fangs of flashy adventurers' bedside rugs.

There was a lion sleeping on its two crossed paws, its black eyelids lowered, which must have been a terrible sight at dusk, for it seemed to be only sleeping. Weapons were crossed above or below the dead heads, savage, curious weapons.

On the floor, a red Smyrna carpet, red currant, winey red with violet, almost black, patterns, spread out a pool of blood or grapes on which one trod with a certain apprehension about possible splashes.[2] And black furniture, glinting with iron-work, gold incrustations, or mother-of-pearl, gleamed in the darkness of the corners or of the draperies. Ebony columns encircled with bronze, with silver, with marble bracelets, held strange idols, from the traditional Buddha, holding up two inflexible fingers, to the *Snake-God* of Oceania, branching and tufted like a tree. Under a dais of Indian muslin, a Brousse silk, iridescent, changing, one minute a very delicate azure blue, the blue of a French sky turning towards green, the next a dark blue spangled with reddish stars, a pile of multicolored cushions and pale satins made up the bed. It was more like a big egg cut in half, an egg of white lacquer full of delicacies riotously colored in paper wrappers of lace. Opposite the bed, emerging from a swan tuffet, a circular divan entirely covered with that miraculous down, stood a black *Eros*, an antique marble statue, with green contours, having no doubt long remained exposed to the biting winds and tears of rain. This Eros must, at one time, have held a metal bow, but his right arm, bent back at eye-level, now displayed only a stump; the hand had gone off with the taut string, and the left arm was completely missing. The child, pitiful and wild at the same time, flashed emerald pupils set in two white cameos and he opened wide, in the middle of his Negro face of regular ferocity, eyes of a real, divine existence.

Léon Reille drew back in the presence of the naked lad who seemed to threaten him with his terrible stump.

"Oh!" he said, "It's horrible! I prefer the pot. At least it's blind. That one must see you as you are."

Eliante began to laugh.

"He certainly does see me, but he can hardly touch me."

Leon held his companion's arm tightly.

"Why did you bring me here? All these beautiful things are hostile towards me. We leave a little garden the color of hope to come into this cavern where I'm suffocating."

"I want you to feel at home here!" she said calmly.

It was the first time she used the familiar form of address. He felt a new thrill. A painful dizziness enveloped him, and he felt like laughing.

He inhaled deeply the air saturated with a perfume by turns fruity and flowery like this woman by turns old and young.

"You're mad, Eliante! Or you're terribly vicious," he murmured. "Yet . . . yes . . . I'm glad about the play you're acting for me. I no longer dread anything except waking up. So I'll try to become more complicated. What do you want from me at this moment, eh?"

Wheedlingly, he bent down, seized the white train of her dress, and rolled himself into it, a little embarrassed at finding himself at the mercy of the arrows. She tried to pull the bottom of her skirt away from him, still smiling.

"I want you to listen to me. . . . When children don't behave, people tell them stories."

"That put you to sleep, right? I'm going to bed, I've had

enough of playing the proper gentleman. If I snore, pull on my sleeve. . . . Eliante, the carpet smells of wild animals? Heavens, that's funny! That smells of wild animals, and, in the air, it smelled of rice powder. I'm losing my head or else we're in the dream about faraway islands!"

Spread out at her feet, all black in his serious young man's clothes, he really looked like the pair to the naked, and chaste, Eros, because of the blackness of the marble.

He did not sleep at all, his eye fastened on the white love prey, ready to pounce if she tried to slip away too ignobly. Would she slip away again? Or was it really him, the prey stalked by the invisible bow of the cruel hunter?

She wanted to play? They would play . . . as cruelly as she wanted, but he had not had his hands cut off. It would end badly.

Eliante sat down on the swan tuffet, became serious again:

"My bedroom," she said, "is just how it was five years ago, on board the *Saint-Maurice*, the big ship my husband captained. Imagine it all, my dear, heaped up in a cabin relatively too narrow, lit by a porthole, an oval cabin like the egg of my bed, and each time we set foot on land we came back loaded with fantastic booty: idols, animal skins, rare furniture, pieces of glassware or very precious stones, poisoned weapons, fabulous fruit, wild flowers. We piled it up in my room in any order, without any sort of attention. It wasn't always clean, the stuff they brought back for me, it smelled of rancid oil, more rancid oil than vetiver. A horrible smell of coconut oil which impregnates everything in tropical countries and everything you touch smears you with a particular grease." (She smelled her hands.) "For all that I live in Paris, when I remember, it turns my stomach! and then there were cargoloads of spices, skins of wine, jars of special liquids which travelled with us to give the sailors what they call *the taste of the sea*. My husband

never found my room full enough, rich enough. He spent outrageous sums collecting things which got ruined, spoiled, and had to be thrown into the sea before returning to France. Above all, he liked idols . . . all the Buddhas you see here are not the most . . . original?" (She hesitated.) "And there are my famous robes, a unique collection of oriental costumes made for me, to order. And the collection of ivories . . . I have to show you everything, don't I?" (Her voice died away suddenly. Léon contemplated her from below, spread out on the white waves of her skirt, he had rested his chin on his palms, and he never took his eyes off her.) "By wanting to know another man . . . besides my husband," she began again, "I owe that man a full confession . . . he already knows who I am, I want him to know equally the one person whose memory alone could forbid me to love . . . "

"Eliante," interrupted Leon, a little worried, "you are talking . . . Chinese! You are mixing up feelings that have nothing to do with each other. Did you love your husband, yes or no? Is it to his memory you want to remain faithful? Which man do you wish to know in me? I've told you what I am: not much! You, you are an adorable creature, very perverse probably, that delights me today; if tomorrow I bitterly regret it, in whatever connection, rest assured that it won't be to you I complain! I have reached the temple, I don't care to leave. Are you then more of a little girl than Missie? And damn it all, Madame Eliante Donalger, can it be you don't know, in practical terms, what your niece professes to know very well in theory? Monsieur Donalger loved you passionately, I'm sure. You hardly returned his love, it wasn't a crime because you were too . . . young for him. At present, your cup overflows . . . you are tired of being a widow . . . offer it to me, that cup, don't worry, I undertake to drain it! I have a thirst capable of leaving an ocean of love dry. So the story about the pot was no joke? You would have liked to fulfill the fine dream of staying chaste . . . by staying in love? That gives you an attack of nerves, madam? He was very good, very generous, this husband, showering you with presents, satisfying all your whims, and, you poor girl, having left a sad convent, you felt remorse at not completely satisfying that man? Am I guessing right? You owe him everything, and you think you also owe him eternal fidelity. I believe, my beautiful Eliante, you are exaggerating. One doesn't love to order, you can't put on real passion like one of your oriental robes. That man might be the best of mortals, you were not bound to adore him for his generosity alone. So show me his portrait before the other things, would you, my . . . friend?"

Eliante stood up. He noticed she was smiling, now, with a strange smile, and the small folds which set her delicate mouth between two parentheses were unusually deep.[3]

"Yes," she said in a dull tone, "I'll show it to you. I should have begun with that."

She turned to a large cabinet incrusted with mother-of-pearl and gold, a piece of dark lacquer with starry reflections, separated into two parts by a twisted shelf imitating the staircase of a pagoda crowded with ornaments. The left panel depicted mountains of ice illuminated by northern lights. Eliante turned a grating key, the mountains of ice disappeared, swallowed up, and fire seemed to leap out from inside the piece, which was lined with red copper. From this flashing sanctuary, she removed a wallet of mauve Morocco leather, opened it, and the medical student couldn't help noticing that the portrait of the deceased was sheltered from indiscretions like an anatomical part.

Leon sat up on his knees, leaning his elbows on Eliante's knees. He was finally going to meet that husband whose memory still *enchanted* his widow; the *other* man, the *dead* enemy of the *newborn* love.

Madame Donalger placed in front of him a large photograph, an officer's head, topped by the low and braided kepi of the navy, his cheeks bearing the traditional whiskers, a stiff collar, a forty-five-year-old face, in which the eyes seemed gentle, the very contemplative eyes of a *water-lover*, but, despite the precautions of the photographer, who had placed his subject under the awning of an antique colonnade, the flaw of this face was immediately apparent and held one's gaze so that one scarcely noticed the rest.

Commander Donalger had lost half of his nose, either by a gunshot or saber cut, or through a machinery accident, a boiler having exploded near him.[4]

Leon made a gesture of pity.

"Poor man!" he murmured.

"It's not very noticeable in this portrait," she said in a dull voice, her hands trembling slightly. "There is an earlier one which one of his friends had drawn on board, at the time of the accident . . . this one."

She passed him a sheet of yellow paper on which was reproduced the same face, only this time, quite horrible. It looked like a caricature, like some macabre joke. The face, cleanshaven, showed a bloody stump where one could distinguish the cartilages forming the opening of the nostrils, which no longer existed except as pulp. Stoically, the lips smiled, intact and mocking, trying to give some presence to the terrifying mask, laughing at his own ugliness, seeming not even to feel it. That sailor was blonder, paler than the official character in the photograph, but, his eyes, copied, without the tricks of touching up, retained a frightening expression of feline ruse. If this younger Donalger was really a brave man, he must hide certain cruelties of character, deep in his courage, forbidding himself to be a brave man.

Leon Reille concluded simply:

"Poor Eliante!"

Out of modesty or disgust, she closed the case once again on both faces.

"Why keep . . . the earlier one?" asked Leon not daring to soften any more.

"He's the one who gave it to me. He often used to say: 'when I am far away, you'll see me this way, and when I come back I won't seem so ugly.' He never wanted to have any device put on his scar: 'since a false nose is inevitably going to come off, I'd rather stay frightening than be ridiculous, even for a minute. A frightening man isn't ridiculous,' he would repeat to me, and I think he was right."

"It is, indeed, a profound insight, but you no doubt would have preferred . . . the false nose, you being such a good actress?"

"I'm not an actress: I'm afraid of love, as I was afraid of my husband, that's all."

"Heavens! Monsieur Donalger has nothing in common with . . . an ordinary lover."

And Leon Reille stopped himself from adding:

"How can he be compared to me, dear madam?"

She smiled, melancholically, a little mysterious in her melancholy, and, going to put away the case, she picked up a little tray on the stair of the pagoda.

"I'm going to make you drink some very special coffee, which I prepare myself," she said in a very natural tone.

He made a face:

"The philtre? Yes, I really need to forget."

She moved a miniature mosaic table closer to him, and set down on it the little tray, which held two imperceptible cups, thimbles, barely filled with a brown essence, in pellets like putty, in which essence she dropped, from high above, a few drops of boiling water. The aroma of the coffee spread very violently around them.

"Drink, monsieur my friend, and dream . . . I'll show

you now the collection of ivories and the one of wax, perhaps my robes, but we won't have time, I'll save them for another occasion."

"It's terribly bitter, your philtre."

Eliante arranged white objects on the red carpet, statuettes which she brought down from their shelf or which she took out of the cabinet. Leon anxiously studied her movements, unable to resign himself to his role as mere spectator.

How gracious and supple she was, this artificial woman, in her high-necked dress, so dressed up that she appeared naked under the white velvet stretched over her without a wrinkle, without any apparent seam! How her body resembled an ivory statue, a somewhat velvety ivory covered with down or snow! And her black helmet, so tight as to cut her delicate ears, her severe features, were lit by the glimmer of her eyes. She was celebrating a sort of religious ceremony, there, in the middle of this temple, where she was truly at home, an idol herself, exultant at the touch of idols.

"Listen to me, Leon," she sighed as though in prayer, "and don't get angry, love frightens me when it's true, and love is always sincere when it springs from all our instincts. We love uniquely in so many different ways. When the god passes over us, by faking love one loves, and by loving one is exasperated not to love more. One arrives at crime easily, logically. It's a path of roses which is stripped, as you ascend towards the summit, of all its flowers. Soon your feet bleed on the stones, are torn by tangled briars.[5] There is no limit for those who wish to ascend to passion, and whoever does not stop along the way goes mad. I don't know if I am a woman one can respect; however I hope, I dare to hope, that you will love me better than my husband was able, or wanted to love me. It will be the same thing, better, purer, closer to god. Henri Donalger was *man par excellence*, I want you to be the hero. No, I didn't love my husband, it's only today that I fear him for you, for he is no more than what he has left in me. I am, perhaps I will always remain his humble servant, or yours. How shall I go about being your mistress? What shall I offer you that has not already belonged to him?" (Eliante kneeling presented to the young man an ivory statuette, a little naked idol, straight in its lines, the elbows bent, the two hands joined together over its genitals.) "Here is a Psyche of the yellow race, Tchun-mei, she who awaits the monster to be tortured by it, and this monster is a marvelous dragon with wings of carbuncles, and three heads. She will die on her wedding night. Look how the poor girl is pure, thin, *childlike*, how she naively parts her hands slightly at the threshold of her sanctuary of love, imitating, despite her virginal innocence, the form of the dear object she wishes to steal from the monster! And her fingers, long and tapering, armed however with claws, with nails as long and tapered as her fingers, are no use for anything except to betray her in the most pitiful way in the world. But," continued Eliante, turning the statuette on the tip of her index finger, "she is not a goddess, alas! she's a woman all right, a little girl, a little schoolgirl torn from her convent, judged ripe for the monster; she is sad and pretty, so thin one would think she were a candle, wax scarcely alive with the life given by the mystical flame of her eyes . . . and you can, can't you, give her a halo?" (The young man, more and more interested, leaned over the statue. He had just noticed that she really did seem to be part of an unusual hallucination. Was it the strong aroma of the coffee, or, worse, did she really resemble Eliante? The little idol seemed to change color, if not form, she became waxen, as she turned, of a substance more colorful than ivory. On one side the divinity, on the other the body, the flesh of a mortal. And the little hands, also slightly open in the shape of pink conch shells over the genitals, defending them or imitating their mysterious lines, seemed less long, possessed less claw-like nails, the nails of . . . a French woman.) "Now I'm going to show you the twin sisters at the right of the god Hi-djin. They are his favorites, but he has many others."

Leon Reille tried to seize the statuette. Eliante pulled it away.

"Give me Mademoiselle Tchun-mei," he shouted impatiently. "I want to know why she is double and why I imagine she resembles you."

"I'll explain it to you in a minute, my dear friend. Mademoiselle Tchun-mei is not the only one of her kind. Here, these are the twin sisters."

Eliante offered him a pretty reclining woman, who seemed to be preparing an acrobatic exercise. Her body was attached to what served as a resting bed only by the base of her neck and her heels. This little woman, adorned with the marks of the dragon, that is to say decorated with a tiara studded with tiny blue and green turquoise gems, no longer hid anything with her long hands, candidly spread apart, on the contrary, and very indicative. Eliante turned the statue around and, again, Leon found another figure, attached to the bed by only her neck and heels. Only the same jewelled tiara served for both of them, one in ivory, the other in wax, and the idol's tiara covered the woman's hair, rising in tiers over her forehead in curls which followed all the twists of the marks of the victorious dragon.

"Now look between the two sisters?" said Eliante.

The outline of the two forms seen back to back, joined only by the neck and heels, produced a shape of awful obscenity.

The dragon was certainly victorious . . . but at what price!

Leon burst out laughing.

"Yours is a very pretty collection, Madame Eliante. Are there any others . . . more incredible?"

"Yes," she murmured in a grave voice. "There are some who don't turn their back on each other. Look."

She held out to him an idol seated on a jade throne, holding the crouching dragon on her shoulders and caressing a horrible little man whose physiognomy was much more that of a monkey than a human being.

"This one is a priestess officiating. You can look at her any way you want, she . . . is busy everywhere."

Leon astounded contemplated the priestess:

"My dear Eliante, it's unspeakable! To think that elephants, poor devils, have been massacred so that people can torture their defenses like this!" (He added, frowning.) "So why does Mademoiselle Tchun-mei look like you? And also one of the twin sisters?"

Eliante, without answering him directly, held out to him a statuette rolled into a large ring, a small wax woman not repeated in ivory. The lengthening of all the limbs was so chaste and so natural, the little enamel eyes were so lively that you expected to see her jump like an animal, unwind like a spring, and, rapidly, Eliante presented the same small woman relaxed, seated, her arms crossed around her knees, her hands joined, all gathered into a new circle, showing with simplicity everything she could show.

Three other wax statuettes varied the pose, presenting in the agile hands of Madame Donalger that same little idol with the luminous enamel eyes, beautiful little eyes so black and so brilliant at the same time. They seemed to multiply, to blossom on the red carpet, all white, all pale with pleasure, impassive little madwomen, frozen in their works of love at the precise moment when they could have enjoyed what was happening to them. And these numerous little wax dolls were modelled with charming art, touched up by brush, delicately enlivened with carmine, as though caressed by a feather dipped in blood. They were so pretty that he who contemplated them had followed their licentious evolutions, with a somewhat scandalized expression, now smiled, quite moved at finding them so pure of form.

"But still, why do they look like you," stammered Leon, resting his index finger on the sweet face of the last one, who, both arms bent above her head, was haloed by a fan, letting a blue dragon clasp her around the middle of her body. "I'm dreaming perhaps . . . that they resemble you?"

"Don't you understand?" murmured Eliante softly. "It's nice of you not to dare to guess, so I must tell you: they resemble me because it's *me* they represent. The double is copied from my own body. The first time my husband saw this idol in a pagoda, in China, he wrote to me, for I hadn't wanted to accompany him yet, that he had just discovered my sister, and, enthusiastic at her discovery, he bought a miniature copy in ivory of the large statue and had a wax one modeled behind her. I must explain that in China the art of sculpting in ivory or any other substance which can be painted in skin tones is at least as widespread as the art of photography here . . : always supposing that it is an art to reproduce nature exactly in full mourning! They, the Chinese, seek to create a nervous sensation. Either they make it horrible or they make it delicious. Thanks to the enthusiastic indications of my husband, for me, they made it delicious. I'm no longer as pretty as that! The twins on the right were cruelly separated, and I replaced the one without the goddess's tiara. The others . . . they came into the world successively, according to Henri's moods, during the long sea-crossings. He modeled the wax himself like a real artist, and, during my absence, his fingers kneaded all these little women in my image. When I travelled with him, he spent hours attending to the heads, giving them my physiognomy, especially my eyes. I didn't always want to go along with his fantasies, because I was far too young to grasp the divine sense. Now, I see that his love went as far as . . . "

"Eroticism," cried Leon Reille, sitting up, revolted. "Your husband was a monomaniac, a dangerous madman, in need of a cold shower!"

This time the young man was sincerely indignant. To play with obscene little goddesses, he had kept his patience, but a jealous furor seized him in front of these emblems of conjugal prostitution.

"What? All that, all these filthy little objects, Madame Eliante! And you've had the audacity to show them to me? Take it all away . . . quickly . . . remove everything, do you hear me, or I shall smash, with one single kick, this whole infernal little world. Ah! he was a fine one, your Henri Donalger. Hide that, you hear me, or it's you I'll smash. I've had enough of this dirt."

Eliante, with a rapid movement, threw the train of her dress over the innocent little goddesses, then she murmured:

"There," she said. "Poor things, it's not their fault! Would you have preferred the lie of silence, Leon?"

He thought for a moment, his forehead in his hands.

"What do I know? You betray me again, in front of me, and . . . with whom? With the memory of a dead man whose hideous mask would make any woman back away?"

"Perhaps I'm not a woman, since I have only ever known that mask of a man."

Suddenly very serious, Eliante looked at him her eyes full of glimmers. She did indeed have the black and pearly eyes, with a luminous fixity, of the little wax figurines.

Leon fell back, onto the white fur of the couch.

"You don't love me Eliante! You will not love me! You're trying to martyr me to make me talk nonsense. At the moment, you see, I would die before I would admit to loving you. I'm ashamed of knowing you."

Imperceptibly, Eliante shrugged, then she began again, very calm, turning towards the Chinese cabinet:

"And you haven't seen everything, my dear little lover, there is still a heap of extraordinary things, from even further away than possible. Here are animals, the monster spider, the *mygale*, who eats the heart of the little Tongchoui, the goddess of darkness, *Calm of winter*, I say heart so as not to offend you; here is the red monkey, who clasps the same little goddess with the closed eyelids, for she is already dead, it's no longer me nor anyone, she belongs to eternity, and finally here is Hoan-hi Koan-mien, the crown of pleasure. You must look at that, I beg you, it tops everything." (Kneeling again before the young man, she presented him, on a large platter of a bluish metal which seemed very heavy, a sort of braided crown of pale flowers with multicolored foliage, now green, now violet, now red and pink, the color of the coral pin which adorned Eliante's head.) "You see! They are women and men twisted together with the dragon, the eternal dragon who represents everything, in this country so old and so spiritual. It is at the same time chimera, this god, demon, sun and moon, it is above all passion! He has a mouth of flames, bloody eyes, claws of gold and wings of carbuncle. As for his immense tail, prehensile and ringed, it fulfills all natural, supernatural, or social functions. Man and woman are spangled with its precious gems. The temples are illuminated by its transparency, and, in front of stores, people modestly hang lanterns! . . . This ivory and jade work is not easily found on open European markets. It was necessary to steal this one from a pagoda, if you can call stealing offering an enormous sum of money to a priest to corrupt him? But, my husband insisted on *his crown of pleasure*?"

Leon Reille examined, horrified. The little men and little women twisted together, no longer able to escape and connected to each other, now by the dragon's mouth, a red mouth, now by the hooked ends of its wings, green claws, now by its long tail, violet or pink, maintained untranslatable expressions of diabolical joy. This little world of painted ivory and translucent jade lived, palpitated, clamored with the complete abandon of all modesty. They were not too odious, these figures, for they seemed to all belong to the same human plant, some monstrous branch blossoming from their mouths, their genitals, as from their jewelled eyes.

"What cannibal king could assume that unworthy crown?" cried Leon.

"But Love alone! My husband! You! Everyone who loves . . . " Eliante answered him calmly.

And as she was about to replace the metal platter in the Chinese cupboard, someone came and knocked on the door of the temple.

"It's my niece," she whispered. "Missie has just returned. Leon, I beg you not to move, to say nothing. She will go away, thinking I have gone out."

The young man fell silent with a gesture of discouragement.

This intrusion of family life was all they needed in such an atmosphere!

He looked at the ceiling, detaching himself from the rest of the adventure.

On the ceiling everything was dark. A thick darkness fell from up there, produced either by clouds of light black material, or by a vault. The rays from the enormous cut topazes of the windows did not shine that far.

Yes, it was indeed night that fell little by little in the brain of the initiate! What to believe? What to conclude? It smelled of wild animal, rice powder, and, in the evening, the shadows took on formidable aspects.

Was the sleeping lion finally going to raise his eyelids?

Or the bear growl?

Or the panthers roar, the tigers pounce?

Too much exoticism!

Eliante Donalger now seemed no more than a beautiful

phantom to him, a vampire with a silvery belly, slipping, swaying . . .

. . . Suddenly she was near him, one of her supple arms surrounded him, and, leaning her face towards his, she kissed him on the lips, and while Missie, imperiously, knocked a second time, he held, pressed against his breast, this woman all fainting with love.

CHAPTER SIX

"I am like a little child naked in a strong wind. I have a fever, I shiver, I'm too hot or too cold. My lips retain the unusual fruity taste of your mouth, and the bitter taste of your saliva lingers on my tongue, making me find everything I eat bland, sickening since nothing is as good as your love.

"I know, I sense that you love me. I would like to deserve the joy and no longer try to steal it. . . . I'll apply myself to following you:

Madame à sa tour monte . . .

Madame à sa tour monte . . .[1]

"As high as I can go, only . . . you see, I'm ill. I have . . . *yellow* fever. I'm jealous, I have nightmares, I have ridiculous visions.

(You have, madam, a strange way of making coffee!)

"I dreamed, last night, that you were like a column of smoke. You started at the center of the globe and touched the clouds. I could see the whole world in its spherical form. You, you kept your face above the column, a waxen face illuminated by pupils of precious stones, and you swayed from left to right,

right to left, in an absolutely intolerable rhythmical motion. And I struggled to reach you the way one struggles, alas! in dreams, remaining immobile. The column you were, always swaying, ended up turning, the folds long veils, those of black dresses, blended into even blacker, thicker smoke, the night of the whole world turned with you in whirlwind gyrations, and it sucked in the clouds, diluted the earth. I was thinking: 'If I fired a revolver into the base of that column, just a powder shot, from a child's pistol, she would collapse because it's well known in sea voyages that a canon shot fired at the base of a whirlwind makes it dissolve into a salutary little rain.' Only I didn't have to hand any revolver or child's pistol suitable for reducing feminine importance. I had to suffer to the point of nausea, to the point of vomiting my soul and its superfluity, to see you playing this trick of the column. . . . My god, madam, how I suffered unnecessarily! and now, tired of turning, your waxen face looked more human, your eyes had charming looks of pity, but you were very distant, for you seemed to diminish in a huge regression. And in an instant you were a woman, of normal height, as big as a doll. However, you seemed to leave me, to leave the world, for your little feet were distinctly placed on *the declivity of the globe*. I held out my arms, calling. Your face, a distant little face of agony, was transparently pale, all illuminated by two stars . . . then, the stars went out, the face was dead, eyelids closed and mouth twisted, your feet left *the declivity of the globe*, and you disappeared . . . completely. There remained the thick night, smoky, a globe that looked like the vulgar globe of a lamp of black crystal. And the stars, through space, to me looked like *appliqué on tulle*. Something even more false than your smoky dresses.

"Madame Eliante, I'm very ill.

"No; all the same, I'm not as ill as all that. I eat and drink, I light cigarettes. I go to the amphitheatre. I read big books. I set, yesterday, a fractured ankle, and, if it isn't entirely woman's importance, I looked at that theatre girl's leg with relative interest. A little dancer, a walk-on at the *Gaité Montparnasse* who broke her foot jumping on the set. You hear! I have her address. Ah! but, no, I don't want to go mad! Moreover, she's very pretty, quite young, much younger than you. Now, she uses funny language . . .

"Probably, the habit I'm acquiring of making someone of your acquaintance tell me stories makes me difficult on the choice of subjects. I'm becoming as idiotic as a high-society man, and I'm shocked by a grammar mistake. Having scarcely skimmed you, I come away from my reading with my brain scrambled, my back burning, swearing no one will catch me at it again, and the moment I come across simpler stories, I declare them to be very boring, bland as the fillers in the local newspaper. I remember that one of my friends, a great lover of new poetry, used to say to me: 'Between ourselves, I'll admit I don't understand a thing of what those poets write . . . only, after the symbolists, I can no longer read the others, it seems to me they are the ones who make grammar mistakes!'

"My own case is more serious. After the fruit of the islands, I can't stand the acidulation of apples. These good Norman women have a disastrous moral effect on me. Can it be I'm finally on the road to wisdom?

" . . . Let's chat a little mouth to mouth, what do you say, Eliante? You really should read certain serious authors, not at all meant for women, certain terrifying chapters about nuns. . . . Medically, persons of your sex who allow themselves the luxury of a *supernatural* physicality—and it's clear that you live as you come—end up with illnesses of which the least horrible is *St. Vitus's dance* . . . if they aren't already suffering complete paralysis. If you care about the pretty suppleness of your limbs, beware, and try to sin like everyone else.

"I would even go further, if your servant doesn't please you, or if he should communicate his own concern at not pleasing, look for another who responds better to your aspirations . . . worldly or theatrical.

"What the devil, I'll undertake to look for him for you willingly! I even prefer this last alternative, I'll choose with the greatest discernment! There's the memory of your husband? If you think they're all like him! No! All men are not crippled. Your husband (if he wasn't already dead, poor man, I would go and wring his neck with pleasure) needed to supplement the insufficiency of his . . . plastic with an overflowing of passion which I would dare qualify as criminal, despite my great distrust of big words. They are rudely depraved, his little wax Eliantes . . . and their elder sister is much too chaste. He has unbalanced the character of a loving woman, he has killed the taste for happiness in you, to replace it with an appetite for renunciation. Unless . . .

"I love you! You're right. You're right slowly, little by little, the way a bird builds its nest . . .

"And you are making your nest in my reason, I feel you pulling off a piece of wool here, a thread of silk there, one of my hairs further on. . . . You will pull everything off! Soon I'll be a little child naked in the strong winter wind . . . and no woman, ugly or beautiful, will want to warm me up in the folds of her skirt!

"You are right because what we ask of the mistresses of our twenty-two years is a little more than sexual appeasement. If you had given yourself the first evening, the next day I would have had the sadness of thinking that . . . it was all the same, at the same time having the normal desire to start all over again . . . *to be finished faster*. At present, everything went well with others . . . the only one I want is you, not for one night, but for the only night of unique love, the one that covers the whole earth with one beat of its black wing. I don't know if I love you really, but I would like to die in your arms to be quite certain to remain there. . . . (For example, no coffin for three, all right? May that nefarious husband no longer take up half my place. Free translation! Give me a *concession in perpetuity* . . . but in a cemetery where I forbid him to stick his nose.) Have you thought about this: your husband's skeleton looks like every other skeleton, and the wound on his face disappears beneath the same patina of horror? Go into this idea thoroughly for me! He has a skeleton like anyone else's! I don't want to offend you with my medical student jokes, my beautiful beloved. I have difficulty swallowing what I prescribe for myself . . . without sugar! You, you have a bed like an easter egg, full of surprises, you can change embroidered cushions, you can vary the lace of your sheets, and you sleep in there like those spoiled children who find again in the morning yesterday's candy, the only difference being there's more of it. Me, I go to sleep my mouth salty with sorrow. It's no good smiling at it and devouring it silently all day long . . . all night. . . . In the morning, it's the same . . . the only difference being there's more of it, like your candy, minus the sugar!

"Eliante, my beloved, you are walking in the autumn of a world . . . and I am arriving for the dawn of the other world! In the name of art, of the love of forms, of colors, of all the silent or speaking graces, turn around, do not go down the stairway of rotten dead leaves . . . give me a sign. The young men of tomorrow want to remember you! I beg you to choose me as an interpreter. I come to ask you for my share of pleasure to affirm *to them*, later, in front of the dissection tables, the fertilizing joy of dream . . . when I will have stopped dreaming.

"For there are, aren't there, women who don't kill the chimera? One can hope, can't one, that there is something besides the eternal disappointment of the morning? If your mouth is perfumed like an unknown fruit, your saliva is bitter like tears I know . . . and I forbid you, I, a doctor, to take your secret with you."

Leon Reille

(White card, azure watermarks.)

"Madame Eliante Donalger begs Monsieur Leon Reille to do her the honor of attending the matinée dance to be held at her home on the 5th of January.

"*Juggling to the piano*."

E.D.

CHAPTER SEVEN

LEON, in black evening dress and a white satin waistcoat, since the affair was a ball for girls, had arrived early, hoping to see *her* a while before the ceremonious entries, but he found only Mademoiselle Marie Chamerot already surrounded by an extremely active group.

"There you are, my dear," said Missie, in the tone of a young girl welcoming a *newcomer* for a game of croquet. "Good! Stand over there, be good and admire me. Eh? I have the *performance* of a first communicant. What a figure!"

She turned on one heel, her skirt of illusory tulle covering a white silk dress, a bouquet of primroses at the waist, another in her hair, well curled with the curling iron and wearing such a low-cut dress that the ribbon shoulder straps fell down over her thin arms. She seemed very happy to meet her friends at home and talked to them about forthcoming delights like someone who is not very well informed.

"Yes, my dears, we're hoping to see Lidot, the big comic singer, he promised, I think, to come as Harlequin to amuse us and then we'll have lunch at small tables, some champagne, the very depths of my aunt's cellar, an indigestible return from the islands."

"We're going to get drunk, then!" said an adorable little person in muslin, without silk underskirts because it's *purer* and simply wearing a Mechlin lace bib, because it's more babyish.

There were about fifteen of them all in white, classmates, school friends, patrons of public nurseries, cyclists, a swarm of butterflies *the color of snow*, delicious snowflakes, some pretty, others less so, some downright ugly, with circles under their eyes, layers of yellow on each side of their nose, rather running to seed, with a decided air to become exceptional women, if no one married them, all armed with diplomas and affecting vulgar language, for grand sentences are a drag, and, between ourselves, one can forget all about Professor Whatshisname; all good girls who like to laugh, little plump bourgeoises or pale offspring, too well nourished, or sickly, madly keen to find a husband without the signs of a large dowry on their costume and resolved to take him honestly by storm.

This swarm of modern butterflies (the old ones, those of the open fields, are of a different white) moved into a large salon where Eliante must have walked an hour or two after the caterers had stopped by. It smelled of island fruit. The large white drapes covering the walls were held back by thick garlands of natural mistletoe, and these garlands made an imaginary clicking of fine pearls run throughout the room, in the brightness of electric bulbs. On the ceiling, Algerian silk, white with satiny stripes, was quilted with tufts of mistletoe, scattering on the cloth which glossed the carpet, green as a trimmed lawn, with other fine pearls which the young people picked up carefully, fearing untimely slips.

Green palms and sprigs of mistletoe alternated in tall crystal vases, and, along the benches of striped Algerian cloth, fabulous fans with white plumes put wings on the décor. The men, all very young, fell into it one by one like beetles into cream, took on the awkward airs of insects whose feet are stuck, and copied Leon Reille, sucking their hats in despair.

The young girls had come alone, dropped off by their mothers or chamber maids on the front steps of the mansion, and they had an open physiognomy. The young men continued to look like they were at a funeral, seemed accompanied by the fear of a possible mother-in-law.

It was Missie who received, keeping Monsieur Donalger the deaf diplomat on her right, and she rapidly took care of her visitors:

"Well, is it really you, my dear Noriac? Oh! how kind. . . . You were tired out, you were saying, the other evening at Mathilde's ball? I see things are going better! Well, Monsieur *Colmans*![1] You will be expressly forbidden to put mustard in the champagne today, we will watch you."

Leon was in torment. He was no longer paddling in cream. It was like quicklime cooling around his feet, chaining him to the floor, turning him into an automaton, obliging him to speak, in a neutral voice, to say bloodless things, to dare only evasive gestures. And he would watch the others dance since he didn't know how or didn't wish to dance.

He ended up running across Missie, asked her quietly if Madame Donalger was ill . . . exactly . . .

"Her? Never in her life! She is too good a mistress of the house. She is preparing surprises for us. Perhaps Lidot hasn't kept his word, and she's sending out for something to replace him . . . perhaps . . . *her juggler*. . . . She must be practicing at the moment. Heavens! You know, she treats us to that highlight once . . . in a blue moon, and it's quite natural she should be busy with it. . . . One is always very afraid . . .

"What? It's she who will . . . *juggle to the piano*?"

Missie made an appropriate face:

"Oh, my dear sir, what can you be thinking! Do you take her for a clown! You'll see . . . what you'll see."

And she turned, disappeared, cutting through the wave of young white girls with all the brutality of a worthy young milkmaid in her dairy.

He told himself he was an idiot. Eliante was an eccentric society woman but too concerned with proper behavior to allow herself such an exercise in public. He went back to gnawing the edge of his hat, while he examined the back of the room, where a harmony group had just appeared. Midway between a platform still veiled in large Algerian curtains, stood a harp all in gold flowering with lily of the valley, forming a question mark on the ramp of an improvised theatre. A girl, an artist, that much could be guessed just from the way she dressed: a white wool peplum, a poor dress, yet so gracious, sat near the harp on an X of green velvet, and on either side of the girl two little boys chubby and curly, one brown-haired one blond, stood respectfully—two angels in front of the madonna—holding tiny tambourines. There was a piano which couldn't been seen, Eliante having long ago condemned the disastrous effect produced by the official presence of this box with its heavy right angles like a station buffet.

"How well she understands feasts of innocence!" thought Leon, marvelling at the exquisite art extending to the slightest details.

And when there fell onto him, from the Algerian ceiling, one of these fine pearls, after which the young dancers ran, he shuddered in spite of himself, as though his hair were wet from a teardrop.

A servant, in white satin livery, which made him look like a very great lord in the midst of other men in black, came and set out chairs, preparing a semi-circle, facing the theatre.

At this signal, the orchestra preluded lightly, gaily, then the great curtains opened onto a décor of snow of a pretty, refreshing artificiality, white hills, Christmas trees, a carpet of crystalline frost, and, suddenly, the enchantment of a tender pink light lit up *Polichinelle*, the comic singer *Lidot* monstrously humpbacked and joyously multicolored. He was given a warm welcome. The young men brightened up, the girls guffawed like children at the Punch and Judy show at the Tuileries.

Lidot sang the most admissible couplets in his repertory, recited some absurd monologues. He was applauded for everything, and called back.

The lords in white satin passed around champagne glasses. Lidot disappeared under the closed curtains. There was an intermission.

During this intermission, Mademoiselle Marie Chamerot played practical jokes, sent around a rumor that, very indisposed, the awaited *juggler* would not appear.

In one group, they proposed dancing.

"How distressing," the old deaf diplomat began again, accompanying his niece everywhere and supporting her with his gestures of disappointment, "if she let us down. . . . We couldn't replace her, not her! . . . "

Leon felt the approach of disappointment, and, curious as a child, he hoped all the same for something better than a comic singer in a hurry to get his social obligation out of the way.

From group to group, he collected only vague pieces of gossip, for he hardly knew this world of young people, rich or poor, dowry seekers, not missing a white ball, where generally one drinks well, the parents of these girls having every interest in taking care of the good matches.

"Hush, hush! . . . It's her!"

The curtains opened on the pretty decor of snow somewhat changed. There was a table in the center, a table covered with the traditional striped cloth of the magician.

More feverish, the waltz grew stronger, a jet of light sprang, the color of sulphur, a stormy flash of lightning, and the juggler appeared immediately, greeted by a thunder of the most obligatory applause, since it was indeed, this time, the mistress of the house who came to entertain, in person, all these children! . . .

Eliante Donalger wore the tight-fitting leotard of the acrobat, a very high-necked leotard of black silk, ending at the neck in the corolla of a dark flower. Only her arms were bare. A belt of black velvet embroidered with diamond stars encircled her thighs, and she was wearing a little white wig, powdered, a clown's wig, ending in a crest under a diamond butterfly. For her modesty, she had put on a velvet mask, and of her skin one could really only see her mouth, very red, her mouth between parentheses . . . on a black and white page!

It smiled, this mouth. That emphasized her dimples. Missie pranced, threw the primroses of her bouquet, and the men, standing, behind her chair, felt seized by the little thrill that takes all men in front of the *form* undisguised despite the disguise.

"Very nice!" murmured someone.

"Be quiet!" shouted Leon Reille, quivering with an anxiety impossible to disguise, that one.

Missie gave him a malicious tap with her fan. Eliante came forward on the side with the table, bowed, and everyone fell silent, because the gesture was serious like the bow of a swashbuckler. There were boys and girls there, scarcely two or three serious men, but you could have heard, now, a fly expire in the milky draperies.

Madame Donalger held herself straight from head to toe like a statue, her breasts swelling the leotard but little, her hips attached high, allowing, without a false movement, an almost masculine appearance.

Leon admired her to the point of suffering. Was she going to torture everyone at once? It would be intolerable! He would go and snatch off her mask to prove to them all that she looked like the little wax dolls, the little ivory dolls? Was she going to juggle with that in front of them? No! he would not allow it! . . .

She picked up, on the table, a dagger with an ebony handle, threw it in the air and let it fall to the ground, where it stuck, still quivering, its steel blade casting blue reflections, then she took another one, made it fly, caught it again, tried its point on her index finger.

So the waltz murmured, in the background, letting the single amorous harp vibrate. Eliante seized all the knives, threw them with a measured movement, caught them in flight successively, making them turn higher, in a diadem of blue flames, above her forehead. She juggled very simply, but really, with heavy knives, quite sharp, and, what would have been ordinary for an artiste at the *Folies-Bergère* or *Olympia*, seemed amazing for a society woman.

She smiled constantly as she followed with her eyes the flaming knives, and her look, under the black mask, shone luminous and solemn, the eyes of a tigress watching the games of her little ones, and who forces herself to show how easy they are to lead in existence.

The knives passed, passed again, flew, and made an unusual metallic sound ring out. Her powerful little hands did not tire of receiving them, of throwing them, of receiving them again, so that for a moment, the rhythm being perfect, they seemed to be turning themselves around a crown of blue flames, a crown of immobile knives.

People applauded. Leon left the joy of the noisy manifestation to his neighbors. Having taken refuge in the last row of guests, he kept for himself the pain of seeing her there, standing and juggling, separated from her family, from society, from the whole world, from all of human society by the enigma of her perpetual comedy.

And he guessed that she was juggling not only in his honor or in their honor, she juggled to please herself. It was as though one could feel another blade both perfidious and passive vibrate in her. She amused herself naively, absolutely, with the unusual pleasure she procured for them, and she needed too the acute desire of the looks focused on her, all the vibration of an atmosphere charged with amorous electricity.

Leon knew how that would end in the wings! She was not one of those actresses who tire after the encore. She would play again, vibrating with the single metallic vibration of her knives, a steel blade tempered in the fires of passions, henceforth disdainful of blood and flesh, using only its own black sheath.

As the waltz became more ardent, Eliante put one knee on the ground, continuing to juggle in this gracious posture of inspiration.

She made the knives pass behind her shoulder with the hesitating little gesture of the child who risks the difficult *bit*, and, at the moment one least expected it, with a chord on the harp, she quickly leaned her head back and received the last knife full in the breast. It went in, seemed to quiver like the first one had quivered in the floor of the platform.

The audience let out a cry of admiration.

Leon shouted in horror, covering his face.

Madame Donalger, solemnly, removed the knife, looked for a pretty little lace handkerchief in her star-spangled velvet belt, then wiped it and, as it should, the handkerchief turned red.

Eliante stood up, bowed.

It was the end, *the highlight*, the new trick one always owes to the regulars.

The girls shouted, threw bouquets, their cheeks quite pink.

The young men, some of whom did not know the *trick*, were a little pale.

A wave of madness made the blood run hotter in the veins, and the white draperies were tinged with pink, imitating the deceptive little handkerchief. The lowered curtains reopened three times.

People stormed the stage, Monsieur Donalger, remembering his young evenings at the opera, offered his arm to his sister-in-law. Missie had an idea.

"A collection, gentlemen, a collection! All your button-holes on the dish!"

Flowers rained onto a large feather fan held by Eliante, who was getting angry, saying she wanted to change costume first.

Arriving in front of Leon Reille, she smiled:

"You don't have a button-hole, do you . . . so . . . give me a coin . . . one little coin with a hole in the middle, mister, that will bring me luck!"

Missie was delighted to see the young man troubled.

"Oh! the big fool has nothing to offer us! So steal some mistletoe! . . . There's no shortage of it, all around you!"

Mechanically, he pulled out his change purse, revealing, among the gold coins, a thinner one, a holy medallion his mother had given him and which he dared not lose because it would have caused a scene . . . in the family (Madame Reille asked to see it once a year, on Easter day.) He threw it on the fan. Eliante picked it up.

"Well, well! A Virgin medallion! Thank you, sir . . . I shall pay you back."

And she bowed solemnly, while Missie pursed her lips. In the gap of the leotard, split above the heart to hold the case which received the knife, he saw white skin, the case was no longer there . . . he closed his eyes.

"I should hope so, madam," he stuttered.

Eliante left the ball to get dressed.

Missie supervised the distribution of the champagne.

The servants put away the chairs.

Leon seeing everyone very busy, the orchestra starting up a quadrille, slipped along a corridor. He knew the way a little, got his bearings, collided with servants carrying refreshments who growled.

What he was trying to do, he didn't really know very well himself. He went down a service staircase all padded with Turkish carpets, reached the bedroom, found no one there, crossed the dining room and bumped into a cathedra, which made a noise falling over.

A door opened, a woman let out a cry of terror. Leon assured himself that she was alone in the little old rose salon.

"Eliante," he whispered, "I've come for the change from my medallion."

Softly though he spoke, she jumped back, seized something shiny on a dressing table, either the diamond butterfly which topped off her wig or one of the knives . . . and threw the knife randomly, with all her strength.

The young man, instinctively, covered his chest with his hat, but his hand was pricked.

"Oh! Eliante! It's me . . . you could have killed me?"

They remained for a second looking at one another, breathing heavily.

The temple in which the great white vase was set up had been transformed into a dressing room, and a huge mirror hid the famous pot.

Eliante began to laugh, nervously, then, without transition, threw herself into the arms of the young man.

"Darling! Darling! I didn't want to do it! I didn't want to hurt you! My dear little love friend. . . . You see, it's stronger than me the idea that I shall be surprised . . . raped . . . I can't bear that."

She hung on his neck, unmasked, uncombed, all enraptured by pleasure and emotion, her face upset, her eyes sparkling.

"Not very nice your fine knife."

He showed her his bloodied hand.

So she busied herself, poured water, waved phials and powder puffs.

"There, it's nothing! I love you! I'm not mean. . . . It's my nerves. Kiss me! Forgive me!" (She pressed her whole body against him, her hands clutching his shoulders, supple as a serpent.) "I'm happy to detain you an instant here and tell you that the party is for you. Did I entertain you, at least?"

"Naturally! A white ball, that suits me completely. I'm so chaste. Ah! don't kiss me, you know, or I'll shout! Missie, your brother-in-law, your heaps of people! I'm absolutely scandalized. Aren't you ashamed to offer yourself to everyone the same day. Are you all right? Tell me? who taught you to juggle, your husband again, no doubt!"

"No . . . " (she pulled up the collar of her leotard), "it was in Java, during a fever I'd caught, in that country. I was bored, Henri had some jugglers come, and I learned, having nothing better to do. I often injured myself, then I ended up really knowing it. You just have to keep up your hand from time to time. You're going to leave, aren't you? I must get dressed, they're waiting for me upstairs."

"Leave . . . as if I wanted to!"

"Come on! Don't give me frights . . . since I love you. Your letter is a good letter . . . you love me too, don't you. I think in the end we'll come to an agreement . . . only . . . I want to have you as a lover . . . when it suits me. . . . Should lovers love each other like . . . spouses? No! it would be ridiculous! there must be a difference! And Missie is watching us! I'm not free and . . . I don't want to hurt anyone any more. . . . My brother-in-law, poor thing, he would die of sorrow."

While saying these things, strange in her juggler's mouth, she was swooning, seized by the odor of the young male who was kissing her neck, and the beauty of their pose being reflected in the clear mirror.

They were very beautiful, very proper, she quite naked under the clinging silk of the leotard, without a corset, without a ribbon tying her limbs, he covered in nuptial satin.

"What do you love about me today?" he asked, wanting to cry with rage, for, decidedly, she was mad.

"I don't know . . . . I think it's this white satin; my nails when they touch it tremble as at the touch of the edge of my knives. And then I feel, I'm certain to be beautiful, to please you. That makes me madly happy."

"You can't imagine anything better? In a word, you're going to make us lose eternity waiting for a more propitious time . . . what time could be better than this?" (And bitterly he added): "Will you be younger, eh, tomorrow, or in a year? Think a little, Eliante, have pity on yourself!"

"Here's the point," she said, shaking her head, "there's the moment or there's eternity. You must choose. . . . In a year, in two years . . . tomorrow perhaps you will see me grow old! I want to pass over your life like a dream and not like a vulgar realization. I know I'm the only one . . . the doctors have told me, and I'm afraid of the love of men which is mortal."

"Egotist!"

"I have the right, for I no longer want to kill."

"Your husband . . . "

"My husband is dead because of me. First, he got worried, had fits of violent trembling, his hands and feet danced on their own; his officers noticed something, one day while he was steering his vessel and . . . I didn't want to accompany him any more. . . . But his worries grew, he had attacks of terrible jealousy, because I was no longer there. He wrote me terrible letters . . . which kept me from sleeping. He fell completely ill, gave his resignation and died at home, senile." (She added in a childish voice): "The little medallion, tell me, where does it come from, Leon?"

"From my mother," Leon answered her, crushed.

"May I keep it? It will protect me from bad luck."

"Of course! what's that got to do with it? Eliante? You're lying! you must be lying . . . why are you lying to me?"

"No, there's a furnace inside me. I'm inhabited by a god."

There was a painful silence.

"Eliante! Will you marry me? Endow your niece with your whole fortune, keep only the knickknacks you like, and come with me. I'll cure you . . . or we'll die trying."

She turned away, arranged her face in front of the mirror.

"Come on, I'm going to get dressed! I'll put something on over my leotard, and we'll go back up together, since you want to stay here."

She took off her velvet belt.

"Here," she said sadly, "give me both your hands . . . and swear to be good . . . it's the doctor I'm talking to."

Looking into his eyes, she placed his hands on her sides. They were burning, and he was so surprised that he didn't even think to smile.

"But, darling, it isn't reasonable. One isn't hot like that when one wants to live alone!"

"One is hot like that when one is *Love* . . . and when one is love one can live alone. Come on, leave . . . "

He didn't go away, his arms hanging.

She got dressed, resigned to not taking off her leotard. She put on a strange outfit, a sort of black velvet jacket, very tight at the waist in the back, opening, at the front, onto a long cascade of yellow sulphur silk gauze. Mixed ruby and amethyst brooches fastened the riding coat over the foamy under layer. Like a good actress who must go back on stage, she redid her face, and, after the last dab of the powder puff, she turned round:

"Look at me! I'm old . . . as old as love, and I feel as young as when I came out of my convent. Do you want to marry me? You are my fiancé? I promise to give you a virgin as reward! That will be the change from your medallion. . . . Come on, your arm . . . and let's escape quickly."

At the ball, Missie was shouting:

"*The wooden horses*, gentlemen![2] Hurry up! Ah! here is Monsieur Reille! Not a minute too soon. . . . I was looking for you. Where is my aunt then? She hasn't come back up? She's a long time at her toilette. We can hardly dance without her."

Eliante, according to *their* convention, entered by another door. People crowded around her, and cornered her. Leon didn't see her again to speak of for the rest of the evening.

At the light meal at small tables, Missie arranged things so as to find herself alone with the young man.

She suspected things.

"We had fun here, today, didn't we, sir? Why do you have such a long face?"

"Great deal of fun, mademoiselle. . . . A day I shall never forget my whole life."

"You say that as though you were about to hang yourself! Do you like the quails in little cases? Pass me the champagne. You're not drinking? It's true you haven't danced, either."

"No thank you, I'm not very thirsty. Or . . . I think I would drink too much, if I drank."

"Ah! Ah! sorrows to drown?"

"No! the noise, the heat . . . "

People were chatting and bursting with laughter around them. Eliante was going from table to table, finding out about needs and whims, saying a gracious word, distributing candy or cakes. Carrying an enormous basket of gilded wickerwork, she seemed to be offering herself, sparkling with jewels and enveloped in light gauze like a beautiful rare fruit in silk paper. She was still juggling! She was always juggling!

Leon's vision was disturbed.

Missie leaned over.

"You find her very beautiful, eh, my aunt Donalger."

"Yes . . . that is to say . . . I find her a little frightening."

"Because she juggles with knives?"

"No," replied Leon getting carried away in spite of himself, "because she juggles with men . . . "

He stopped, confused, his eyes suddenly lowered. He was talking in the presence of a girl.

Missie pouted.

"I understand . . . you're in love with her, *you too*!"

The response was so brutal that he completely forgot his role of good naive young man.

"There are many, then, who court her, mademoiselle?"

"Many, that depends! She lets them come for me, at first. It's a question of marrying me. Then, she does everything she can to . . . pinch them from me . . . for I'm of your opinion, she isn't bad, my aunt, only all the same, she's forty, you know!"

Leon staggered. It seemed to him his glass of champagne contained gall.

"But," continued Missie briskly, getting more animated as she ate, with a light perspiration pearling at the roots of her hair, "she'd be a lot better if she would wear a corset, she'd be *my* size. She has some funny habits! She sleeps until noon, eats cakes and fruit all day and only drinks pure water! No doubt to preserve her complexion. Even so, she wears too much makeup. These creoles are only ever half Parisian women, provincial French women. In the street, people turn and look at her like a *tart*."

Leon shuddered at each word stinging him like a whiplash, a whiplash from a cart driver. This big girl spoke heavily, had abandoned the voice of a schoolgirl on break, and one finally saw the positive woman she would be once married, that is to say, victorious. Ah! that one scarcely bothered to flatter the dreamers or put them to sleep by telling them nice Oriental stories! She got right to the point.

Leon forced himself to smile, thinking:

"This is indeed the virtuous person of whom Eliante said in one of her letters: . . . *she isn't cruel, oh no! she finishes off the little cats she steps on!* And that girl didn't have a penny, lived off the generosity of Madame Donalger, who treated her like her own child. At least if the brother-in-law was a glutton, he knew to stay deaf at the right times."

"Indeed, mademoiselle," whispered Leon disconcerted, "she must often be taken for . . . something she isn't."[3]

"Huh! Neither my uncle, nor I, nor anyone, we'll never know what she really is. She goes out when she wants to, does whatever pleases her and doesn't consult us. She stays as closed as her room. As for me, I'm very glad to have my teaching diplomas, that could be useful one day."

"What do you mean?"

"If she remarried, we could seek our fortune elsewhere, even though we have our rights!" (Missie broke off to suck a mandarin orange and spit the seeds on her plate with a crude movement of her mouth which revealed her gums.) "Yes, sir, I'm philosophical, I've given up on the future. I won't appeal, a lawyer advised me not to, because Eliante received her fortune as a dowry when she got married. Nothing to be done, naturally. But I've received, myself, a fair amount of education, and, by perfecting my singing or piano playing, I can give lessons. Today, a girl is no longer at the mercy of her relations, she is free. . . . Listen, in the public nursery that these young ladies and I founded, I can place myself in the capacity of assistant director whenever I want, and earn three thousand francs a year . . . with the lessons as well, I think a household could manage just as well. . . . So long as one is young, things always work out. A husband *buying* you on your wedding day. . . . Ugh! It's vile! There are some things which shouldn't be bought. Everyone earns their own living, that's all!"

"One buys, indeed, only . . . luxury goods," murmured Leon, a little enlivened by this verbiage of pure reason. "You wish to separate yourself from Madame Donalger, you're wrong. She may need you."

"Come on! Eliante is a pathological case, she's a nervous woman, superstitious, a little mad, but she isn't ill in the true sense of the word. She cries over salt spilled on the tablecloth, and she's afraid someone will break a mirror . . . or a pot, but she's solid as a brick." (She lowered her voice.) "She made her husband so unhappy with all her whims that he died of it. One minute she wanted to follow him, the next she refused to accompany him. I heard from an old negro woman, whom we had to get rid of because she was very dirty, *that Madame was so gentle she was like a mummy*. Women of the world . . . the backward world, who never know how to behave, oppose you always with the force of inertia: 'I'm weak!' 'I have small hands!' 'I'm lazy!' A heap of whimsical pretexts. And the men go completely off the rails."

Leon, now, was drinking milk. By skillfully making this positive young person prattle, one would have all the information one wanted, and one could sort it all out.

"Monsieur Henri Donalger was endowed with a repulsive physiognomy?" he asked.

"Him? His nose was a touch deformed, a small wound of no significance, for which he received a large sum, dear sir. A trifle! It is claimed, on the contrary, that he was very seductive, a talker, a dancer . . . like all naval officers, and he showered her with jewels and extravagant dresses."

"You would willingly marry such a man yourself?"

"Me . . . well, I'll marry anyone to get out of here, where I'm not at home."

Leon, biting his lips, poured her some champagne carefully.

"What if Madame Donalger heard us, she who gives balls in your honor?"

"She would do better to grant me a dowry with her lawyer!"

"Calm down, my dear child. Don't shout such a thing, good Lord!"

"Oh! I know perfectly well that you won't go repeating to her . . . you're starting to do like the other one, who left, one day, in the middle of a reception, slamming the doors! He wanted to marry me. He thought I was the one with the fortune, and, *naturally*, he preferred me to Eliante; but, when he discovered the truth, he fled. A gentleman of thirty-six, besides much too old for me. And that madwoman Eliante had the nerve to say to me that I had shown myself to be too . . . *schoolmarmish* for him. You can imagine how we laughed, my uncle and I!"

"I can quite believe it, it's hilarious!"

"He jilted her . . . old friend!"

"Sorry," said Leon suffocating, noting that, decidedly, modern women did not know how to drink, "it's not her he jilted . . . it seems."

"Oh! she sent him packing . . . in a word, we didn't see him again. A charming fellow, only stuck up . . . "

"But not stood up?" ventured Leon, who was ending up imagining that he was chatting at home with a friend from the clinic.

"Ah! how funny you are . . . yes, that's it, old friend, he didn't get stood up. . . . No! Thank you, I have had enough champagne. Things are starting to turn a little, you know! . . . Will you look at young Juliette Noret over there, she's drunk. . . . Well, if her mother saw her in that state . . . and that ape Edouard who has put bits of paper down her back! No . . . what a good time we're having today."

"A feast, Mademoiselle Marie! We couldn't have a better time if it was your wedding . . . let's hope you'll get married this winter."

"It's quite possible . . . but I'm not a coquette, you know . . . I don't understand what you mean to insinuate?"

"Coquette? No. It's madame your aunt who is that, alas!"

Missie examined him; her watery eye, all drowned in champagne, took on a ferocious expression.

"You think it isn't clear, her existence, eh?"

"I'd never dare affirm anything, mademoiselle, about Madame Donalger, I'm quite certain she is a decent woman . . . of a new kind."

"One is only a decent woman," said Missie in a hard voice, "when one prevents others from suffering."

Leon contemplated her, sighing:

"*In vino veritas*!"

But he kept himself from helping her out with the Latin, for she probably knew how to speak ill in that language, modern and ancient women having the sad habit of using all the means at their disposal to satisfy their bad passions.

"So, you'll come to my wedding?" asked Missie Chamerot, softening once again. "That's kind . . . that's very kind . . . I'll give you my bouquet . . . unless you marry my aunt . . . then . . . well, you'd be my uncle . . . "

"That would seem in order . . . only I don't want to marry anyone, mademoiselle, I'm poor and I don't even have a guaranteed position."

"Bah! a fine boy like you! You can console yourself for anything."

"Too kind, mademoiselle . . . I'm already quite consoled, if it please you."

He threw out this banal phrase, heedlessly, flattered in his young male's vanity, but not at all distracted from his passion for the other, the *mysterious one*. This one, now, he knew her by heart. The other . . . he would think. There remained the famous spring of jealousy! A woman like her could scorn the neighborhood girls. She would perhaps be afraid of her niece.

Then, they got up from the table, Missie leaning on the young man's arm and laughing nervously. He, trying to be nice.

They formed, the two of them, the conventional handsome couple in the sense that they were as tall as each other, as childlike, with thin shoulders, long arms, the same warmth of complexion, a little sunburnt with a few freckles, but, in their eyes the difference burst out and in their movements the hostility of the races showed through. One, coming from an ancient provincial bourgeois mother, austere, both modest and passionate at the same time, selfishly hiding her heart, miserly in its best sentiments, and laughing at herself to hide a painful pride. The other, born of a suburban bourgeoise, a little coarse, quarrelsome, drunk on her recent freedom, new at everything, working at random, and piling up popularizers in the bottom of her memory to vulgarize more without much gain, so athirst for pleasure, for comfort and to make a splash that she always forgets to wash her hands to reach out for it, and, in summary, declaring herself content with the *little* which would have made the fortunes of all our grandmothers.

Leon walked with his feet close together, in a slide both smooth and troubled at the same time. Pleasure led him on, and upbringing held him back.

Missie waddled, strutted like a duck.

She was free.

When one is badly brought up from mother to daughter, one generally has that air . . . and it's freedom which is least lacking.

They passed, very united in appearance, in front of Eliante.

"You should dance the last waltz, my children," said Madame Donalger, who was fanning herself while watching the rapid removal of the small tables.

The harp sighed dying chords. A few couples were turning despite numerous departures.

Leon stiffened:

"Sorry!" he replied brusquely, "I injured myself, a clumsy thing, with a knife, just now—I really couldn't support even the lightest partner."

He braved her with a handsome, proud look.

But Missie intervened, annoyingly eager:

"You don't know how, anyway! It's stupid to not know how at your age! My aunt will show you. It's she who taught me."

"Personally, mademoiselle, I don't want anyone to show me."

"What stubbornness! Eh, my aunt? Invite him!"

He bowed, thanked them and reached the exit, fearing Eliante's mysterious smile. She had added nothing. Besides, everyone was bowing, thanking, taking their leave. The hallway was full of young people, who exchanged joyful remarks along with their overcoats.

Leon made a mistake, put on a garment much too short.

He grumbled:

"Not only mistaking my person, but in addition they lose my overcoat! What a strange house! I've had enough!"

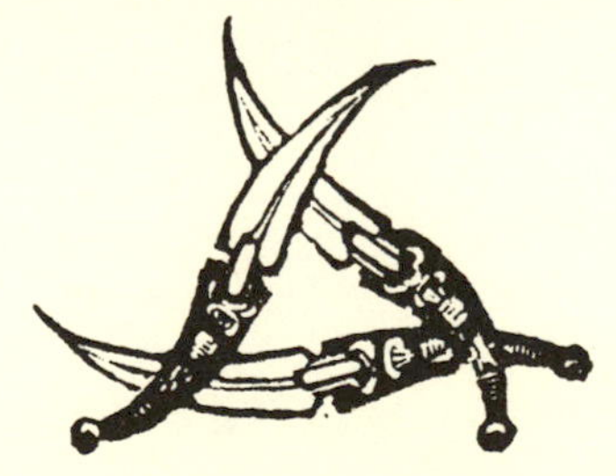

CHAPTER EIGHT

"MY friend, my beloved, my dear little lover, Mr. Fiancé, soon to be the husband of my niece, consequently, *my nephew*!

"I am writing you my first and last love letter:

"I love you. I love you." [1]

Eliante Donalger.

"P.S. .... ?"

E.D.

"My dear Eliante,

"I am answering you, for my part, with my first and last insult letter:

"You bore me . . . "

Leon Reille.

"P.S. . . . to tears!"

L.R.

"My darling,

"Since you are crying, *there is hope*, and I only regret not seeing it, because that would make me very happy! I am telling you things without embellishing them with phrases, and I do not really know how to go about consoling you, but I know all the same that I shall console you . . . for *Love* consoles for no longer loving.

"I think you no longer love me. All it took was for a girl, in a bit too much of a hurry, to court you for what one calls the right reason and to talk to you about me in modern terms . . . you immediately realized that I bored you! So, I bore you, me, the *beautiful juggler*, the *false woman*, the *actress*! And it is my great regret . . . I would like to amuse you, on the contrary, to surround you with pretty flowers, with *real* women, with wholesome smiles . . . also with my arms, for, if they are very white, it is to serve you, darling!

"I had foreseen this eclipse of our star, I am not surprised by it. What I would really like to know is in what terms the child talked to you about me? I would be hurt to be hated by her. I think she loves me or that she will love me one day, sincerely. But, both of you, you are ignorant of the art of loving . . . which is to wait for the right moment. She, chastely—I maintain she is very innocent—you, brutally, you both want to subdue me, to make of me a very docile horse that will carry you at your pleasure, overcome obstacles under lashes of the whip and that you will abandon in the middle of empty fields, *toward evening*, when you return to your houses with happiness.

"I have never had a house, and I have never entered, with happiness, under a really hospitable roof.

"I am the opportunist who passes, dances and picks up sequins with which to decorate her dress.

"I asked you for nothing . . . except to let me dance.

"So you do not want to? You will both be cruelly punished for it. I shall force you to be happy *together* . . . and when you enter your house . . . you will find the sequins there, but the dancer will have left.

"She was, you will say to one another, a somewhat disconcerting madwoman!"

"*The madwoman in the attic*, my children . . . and you will see, despite the beauty of the duty to be united, that one cannot live, young or old, chaste or sensuous, without this madwoman. I think you will both be mistaken.

"As for me, you will not betray me. I am too much *in love* to let myself be betrayed. You will love me, in spite of yourselves, always!

When my husband died, five years ago, I took in, without being obligated by any law, a poor fellow who was dying of hunger because he had been too greedy,[2] and I said to him: 'eat, drink, stay warm, you bear the name of the one who gave me everything, I owe you everything!' I sent for, on his directions, a girl of fifteen, the child of his sister, Madame Chamerot, who had been placed as an apprentice to a milliner, and I said to this poorly brought-up young girl, *an errand-girl*[3] at heart: 'Instead of making hats, you will buy them to put on your head and you will try to forget your former wretchedness, with your workshop words by becoming educated.' These people owe me nothing . . . if they are happy (and I believe my brother-in-law, so long as there is champagne from the Indies will be very happy), but I still owe them everything, a second time, if they suffer on my account.

"You understand, my darling, I am a gentle being . . . very conscious of my actions. No torture of the soul, no joy of the body is unknown to me, and it is quite the least that having silently touched, in the mystery of my divinity, the depths of pain and the depths of pleasure, that I should be able to preserve my friends, my children, from the worst disappointment which would be to realize finally . . . that they will never be gods! If you possessed me, some of you, you would be too jealous of me . . . you would be like my husband, the poor dear man, who used to say: 'She will be happy only by my will . . . or I shall kill her!'

"He died of it!

"I am neither cruel, nor mean, nor just *proud* in the modern manner. I humble myself as people wish and when they wish. At a sign from children who approach me (and all the men who approach me, out of curiosity or as despots, they are just my *children*), I juggle to amuse them, and, if they cry, I cradle them . . . while telling them beautiful stories. I must be pardoned for being . . . happy. But no one will ever know that I carry within myself the great torch of light, the fire which made the saints, the martyrs and the great courtesans, not those who were paid, those who paid for their right to respect by inspiring love! I want, yes darling, to be happy all alone, my arms tightly folded across my breast, my thighs hermetically joined, with the smile of communing virgins.[4]

"What better could you wish to teach me, o my dear little children, who jerk around without dignity like puppets hanging on the same string?

"And yet, because I am without doubt mortal, I have the troubling desire to do good, to please, to communicate my warmth, to still be very beautiful sometimes to inspire a taste for beauty. I know that these times are not fertile in grace . . . I am afraid that tomorrow the grace of woman . . . may be recognized as a *public utility* and be *socialized* to the point of becoming a banal article, a bazaar object like in '93[5] and that one will find types of tender or amusing women with millions of copies like the creations of the big . . . *fashion stores* where it is always the same thing. I want to affirm the superiority of the god over that of the organizer of concerts for the poor.

"Beautiful music is not made for the poor. It exasperates

them, and that which would charm a snake generally makes a minor office clerk sneeze during *grand recitals*. One can be within the grasp of all when one resigns oneself to lower oneself. Why should I lower myself? . . . if I do not need you. It is you who must raise yourself up to me if you desire me. I thought for a moment that *I would raise* a man in the appreciation of my kind of beauty, that a child would come to me truly born of my love and *resembling me*. That I would be able to perpetuate the madness of pleasure . . . to the point of turning it into some happiness allowed by the crowds. So much for that! The gods are alone, and when they stroll, by chance, on earth, they are *pathological cases* or *buffoons, histrions* . . . who are despised!

"They laugh about it . . . in the silence of their regained divinity, all doors closed.

"My dear little friend, my child, you whom I *recognized* at once as a seeker of the god, must you be afraid of me?

"Must you listen to the women of today, my worst enemies?

"They are born tired, today, the granddaughters of reason, and they reason . . . too much.

" . . . Just as the grandsons of my love stray, the men who are reduced to sharing their flesh among these women. For some, pleasure without conscience, for others friendship without passion.

"Goodnight, my little children, amuse yourselves without me!

"For me, I keep everything, I carry everything away . . . I am your dream . . .

"Divine love in an era where there is no more god.

"Love which burns in an era where the world is cooling down.

" . . . Listen, little Leon, I did not want to tell you these things, but I sense that *I will not last and I must use my time well*, I am grieved that, from the first shock of life against me, the jolt of a quite banal reality against a sweet illusion, you revolt and you look at me as one would look at a stranger.

"Ah! that gaze, at the end of that white ball? I am as simple in spirit as I am complicated in body . . . perhaps I am even simple in both aspects. I did not have any jealousy seeing you talk in Missie's ear, I thought: 'He is wrong to give hope . . . for it is a crime to have the appearance of promising a love one will not give.' Take good note, I pray you, that I showed myself, from the beginning, with respect to you as I was. You pleased me, I wanted to love you, I chose you as you seemed to choose me, and I told you: 'If I become your mistress, it will mean that I shall love you less.' I cannot yet resign myself to loving you less! There is my only crime.

"And already you try to prove to me that you are well received elsewhere if I do not receive you.

"And already . . . you do worse, you rouse my born enemy, the vulgar woman . . . *the decent woman*, she who will produce your own unhappiness and your children. Take care, Leon . . . when all is said and done, I can depart into dreams of faraway islands *without you*. . . . I wanted to carry you off . . . with my secret.

"You have not understood?

"You are in such a hurry.

"I am then so old?

"So, let us have this courage to separate immediately . . . or to each of us espouse our ideal.

"You, a girl who loves you. (She will love you, I am sure of it.)

"Me . . . the land where one is warm . . .

"You see, darling, help me to free myself from my last social links. I have the care of a virgin soul. Take it, it will be what you make it. And the envelope of that soul will become according to your taste . . . if you can love it . . . in memory of me.

"Your Eliante . . . who waits."

E.D.

"P.S.—Do not play the proper gentleman, will you?

"Dear madam,

"It is obvious you certainly know the art of love letters just as you know the art of juggling with *chinoiseries* or with knives.

"I am really touched by the trouble you seem to take on the subject of my future, but I prefer to take care of it later, on my own. The girl of whom we are speaking is charming (so well brought up!), unfortunately, I am not looking for a woman . . . to marry."

Your devoted servant
Leon Reille

"P.S.—Now, you can continue juggling from afar. It amuses me very much. If you really thought half of what you say, it would be you I would marry. But how many letters have you written in this . . . lofty style and to how many men *at the same time*? You are *Madam Furnace*, and I have absolutely no confidence in your . . . burning virtue. There are too many *nights* on your dress. Perhaps you never take it off, that black dress, only, if you sleep in it, it is the better to show up the whiteness of your skin, and that's hardly clean, my darling."

L.R.

"Poor dear little beloved,

"No, you are not the only one who dares to say: *the decent woman is the one who gives in*. You have all invented that from your cradle for the greater convenience of your future bedrooms, and you have repeated it so often that the most silly women believe it, today, having finally got rid of some divine prejudices. They are born believing it too, and one hears even *charming* girls declare, their fists in the air, that they will concede, given the chance, in order to assure themselves eternally of rights which are acquired only with a diabolical experience. I know men much better than women, but I never dare undertake anything against the liberty of a man, carnally speaking. That seems to me a crime, and I do not want to be happy at the cost of a crime.

"I know men . . . yes . . . they all want the same thing.

"I know women less, *they do not know what they want*.[6]

"And that is why . . . I forgive them.

"So I must juggle from afar?

"I consent. I am going to tell you the story of my *real* first love letter.

"Well! that first letter *fell into the water*!

"I was supposed to write it to . . . my husband, during the time he stayed in China, after our marriage, not having been able to accompany him because I was unwell.

"At that time, I resembled a wild little cat that one could have crushed by walking on it, without meaning to, and I would often wish that someone would finish me off, because I could not imagine that such was *happiness*.

"However, I believed quite tenderly that one had to love one's husband, and I resolved to write to him, as he had ordered me to do.

"It was on a beautiful spring day (like the beginning of a novel) my window opened onto a garden filled with roses, a beautiful garden out of the fairy tales of Perrault, illustrated by Gustave Doré. The bees entered, went, came, perfume under their legs, and they traced golden signs around me, humming to me to go outside, to run, to gather the flowers and take advantage of my freedom to make as rapidly as possible . . . the bitter honey of experience! I was, at that time, eighteen years old.

"Ninaude, my old negro servant, laying curled up on the ground, began to snore from time to time to tell me that all was calm, that all would be silent, even her devotion, if I wanted to go out and attempt the flight to the unknown.

"I looked lazily at the blue sky, the roses and the black skin of Ninaude.

"I said to myself: *I have to think of my husband*! I began to think heaps of funny things at once. It is amazing how they came to me naturally, the funny things. And it all hung together so badly! It was just like when one prepared a general confession at the convent, we never failed to remember . . . *what we didn't mean to say*! Good Lord! A love letter? How difficult it is to do, and I was supposed to send him a beautiful letter, he had told me: 'My Eliante, you will write . . . a beautiful letter, full of kisses, you will write me all that you do not yet want to tell me, you will write . . . *remembering*!" Yes, I remembered, only, one does not write those things.

"With a big kick, I woke Ninaude who was snoring too much.

"'My little mada, she be hungry?'

"She was still dreaming about the convent.

"'Or thirsty, my little mada?'

"She opened big terrified eyes.

"'No, Ninaude, sing me a song. . . . I'm bored!'

"And I leaned my elbows on my paper so as to no longer think about that paper of despair the color of hope.

"Ninaude sat *tailor-style*, brushed away the flies that were running all over her (I must admit she was a bit dirty and always had splashes of sugar on her), smoothed out her kerchief and without further ado sang:

'Me, little nigger
Love this Missy
Dream 'bout her lips
Want her . . . '

"(Taken in that sense, the name of this animal must not be said out loud, must it?)

'Dance for her
Like a lost soul, alas
Think she's beautiful
Show my . . . '

"(That also begins with an *a*, and it rhymes . . .)

"All Ninaude's songs were in this vein. I cannot tell you the impression that made on me to see the old negress squatting solemnly like a buddha, very properly seated on her heels and singing crazy things with the serenity of one who is telling her beads. She sang in a half-voice because I made her be quiet . . . just in time, but she suspected so little the effect produced that she would have shouted the most scabrous couplets.

"I laughed and laughed, nervously, I cried from laughing. She did not understand, not knowing very well the value of the French words. Nothing was funny for her, only, stupefied, she shook her head.

"'Good that, laughter, for little mistress . . . that will chase the humors out of her body.'

"My husband brutalized her. She sang behind his back, did not complain about the blows from the cane. To stay with me she would have swallowed iron.

"'Good that, the blows, mistress, to chase the humors out of my body!'

"That day of the letter, Ninaude paraded all her rosary of

horrors, there were some so extravagant that I covered my ears, especially since I began to understand them better. I must tell you that Ninaude was my last family. She had been brought back from Martinique, and, in the Paris convent, she took care of me, for Mummy had left a huge sum when she died for me to be raised well. The good nuns let us die of hunger, but we each had our chamber maid. Mine, Ninaude who was nicknamed *Coffee*, prevented us from falling asleep standing up at the main prayers because of her strange devotion. Picture it, she would roll on the ground for the *love of God*, she would cry out, about anything: *It's my very great fault*! I had explained to her that the nuns took a dim view of her and that they might very well end up depriving me of a chamber maid who smelled of *fetishism* (unusual odor; a mixture of musk, sweat, coconut oil and rum!). Full of an extraordinary fervor, *Coffee-Ninaude* implored the holy Virgin by emitting the cries of a wild goose and rolling her white eyes while mixing in all the names on the calendar which she deformed as she pleased, a mixture in which even the devil would not have recognized himself! There was above all a Saint *Firmousse* or *Frigousse* whom we could not admit to the collection. Saint Frigousse had as special mission to give boys to pregnant women. That did not concern us, but that intrigued us, and it was necessary to pray to Saint Frigousse for heaps of other reasons (fortunately): migraines, chilblains, the destruction of vermin, lost handkerchiefs, etc. And naturally he had his song or his complaint, which began thus:

'Saint Frigousse
By my blunderbuss!'

"An appalling hackneyed song of drunken sailors that Ninaude knew in its entirety . . . with variations!

"You think perhaps that Ninaude knew only dirty stories, as filthy as her madras? No, she knew folk legends that

make you cry, and those that make you afraid, her black soul contained equal measures of mud and marvelous precious stones. If she has endowed me with quite a few superstitions since my childhood, she spoke to me sometimes like a book. She was very old and informed us about things forgotten in her country or in ours.

" . . . When Ninaude had sung her entire repertory, I stopped laughing, and I fell back on my paper, discouraged. I was haunted by baroque ideas having nothing to do with love, I wanted to confess, admit my imaginary sins, tell him that, despite his prohibition, I let Ninaude tell me stories all day long.

"Then, all of a sudden, my heart broke in my breast, I began to cry because I had laughed too much.

"Ninaude, still squatting on the ground, crawled up to me and kissed my knees.

"'Little mada, he is unhappy then?'

"And she rocked me while rocking her big black head—where there were probably fleas—in my dress.

"'Yes, Ninaude, I am unhappy, I realize that I cannot write to my husband: I am too stupid.'

"'Poor little mada!' (And her kind eyes like a dog's shone with shrewdness.) 'That is not it! Little mada is not stupid! little mada is like a bouquet I dare not smell; but, if she wanted, I would indeed tell her why she cannot talk to the paper . . . it is because she is afraid of Mr. Officer!'

"'Yes, Ninaude! I am much more afraid of him now that he is gone!'

"'Oh! He will come back,' she said sighing, 'he will come back . . . do not torment yourself . . . and little mada will be a lot more unhappy.'

"'What can I do, Ninaude. I still have to write him a beautiful love letter, he is so good! All the same he left us together, and he could have dismissed you, before leaving.'

"'Yes, my little mada, he is a good Mr. Officer, only the *big red monkey* has pinched his nose in its claws, and that is what torments you.'

"'No! It is not that, you are silly, Ninaude, with your *big red monkey*!'

"This monkey represented for Ninaude fire, gunshots, and generally everything connected to war.

"'Yes, my little mada, I am very silly, it is quite true.'

"Fatalistic, Ninaude sighed, acquiescing with a gesture.

"And my letter did not progress by one line.

"Finally Ninaude, scratching furiously, came across a brilliant idea, along with a flea.

"She got up to go and kill her flea far away from me, and she stretched out her arm in the direction of the garden.

"'Little mada,' she cried, 'look out of the window! It is springtime in France, isn't it, there are roses, there is sunshine, there is a warm sky. You must write him all that and tell him that you love all that *because it is his image*, that you are happy to see him in it now that he is far away . . . That will please him.'

"'So, dictate to me, Ninaude, I am so lazy, yes, that is an idea, make up a kind of song for him.'

"Immediately (one would have thought Ninaude was drinking rum) she began to talk, to talk nonstop, I could not follow her, even galloping with my new pen. She told stupefying stories, calling him one minute *Mr. Officer*, the next *my darling dear*, and the flowers, the kisses, the red monkeys of which one must beware, the big green pearl necklaces he would bring back for me, sugar, rice, liqueurs, all that cascaded together in a swirl of passionate phrases. The letter ended by placing him under the special protection of Saint Frigousse, who would certainly give him a boy one of these days.

"As for me, I wrote, overcome by vertigo, whitening a

little the light turns of phrase; I *translated*, and it was one of the most curious collaborations.

"I reread my missive punctuating it and adding some capital letters.

"It held together, but it was somewhat incendiary, a real letter for the tropics! It left by the evening post beneath a handsome dark green seal with my father's arms. What a relief! my spirit was at rest. My duty was done.

"Ninaude and I, we calculated, on our fingers, that it would take six weeks for the glorious sealed envelope to reach him, counting the train journey, to the vessel the *Californian*, the closest transportation . . .

"This love letter, the first I wrote . . . and which I had not *thought*, never arrived at its destination . . . *because the vessel* the Californian *never entered a Chinese port* . . . it was lost with all hands on a reef, it sunk *with my letter*!

"One must never lie, Leon, in love the smallest lie brings down the greatest vessel and the lives of many good people!

"That, *my dear fiancé*, is the story of the letter that my servant Ninaude had dictated to your servant, but that I made the mistake of not knowing how to write myself.

"When are you coming?"

Eliante Donalger.

"P.S.—I beg you to be the proper gentleman, I have a *day*, do not forget it!"

"No, I do not want to live this way, Eliante! Now it is my turn to lie, to juggle! You have a nerve!

"At a distance, you arrange yourself in such a way as to prove to me that you are a sick child, crying with love in a corner, and when I go to see you, on your *days*, I find a beautiful, very dignified Madam, who offers me her niece in marriage!

"And then, there is the décor! You feed me a *Californian* line! You are a bit too much.

"You leave me the time to think, so I puzzle over my subject, I study my fever—for I have a fever—and I discover that your juggling has the same effect on me as the coquetry of an old woman who is afraid of giving herself . . . undressed! You surround yourself with such a wealth of precautions that I end up wondering what is beneath it. I continue to not want to admit love, or pleasure, in their pure state. What the devil, I am a doctor, or quite close to being one, and I am becoming as doubting as Saint Thomas.

"Your dear niece, could she be right?

"Wait! There is a way to cure me! Come and show yourself at my apartment, disguised as a woman of forty, in the broad daylight of my fifth floor. After, I agree to marry Mademoiselle Chamerot, so as to respect you all my life."

Leon Reille.

CHAPTER NINE

IT was three o'clock when she rang discreetly at his door. He came to open it, not thinking in the least, of her, his mind very preoccupied by the molding of an anatomical piece, a curious deformity of the ear presenting the exact circumvolutions of the shell called *auricula*, half flesh, half conch, and he was wondering if man before the flood . . .

"*Man is descended from the octopus*. Unless it's the oyster! By thunder, who is going to disturb me to smoke all my tobacco while telling me idiotic things?"

"Here I am," she said simply. "I have come to see you, while passing by in this neighborhood *because the weather is fine*. We're leaving behind the mists of winter, spring is advancing, and I had to talk to you about Missie. I am her mother a bit, aren't I? so I supposed you would willingly see me for her sake. I bring broad daylight, dear sir."

She pronounced these terrible phrases without any difficulty, in a calm tone, her eyes confident, although barely open. She always blinked, in front of large bay windows without curtains, and in Leon's room, there was a very large one, overlooking the treetops, the Luxembourg Gardens.

Leon stepped back, a rush of blood in his heart.

The woman who presented herself at his door did not resemble Eliante. She was not even Madame Donalger, she was . . . the widow of a naval officer, someone who must have been very pretty and retained elegant tastes, because they are habits difficult to lose.

For that woman to have dared to come, the Eliante of love, the Eliante of dreams, must have died.

But who then had killed her? Or better still, had she ever existed? Yet another horrible juggling act, unless . . .

No doubt, she was no longer juggling!

Leon felt a veritable spasm of pain.

"Madam," he stuttered, his fingers spread out, all white with plaster and unable to shake her hand, "Thank you for your visit, I wasn't expecting it, no, I would never have believed . . . well, I'm very glad . . . to receive you at my house. You must excuse this disorder . . . and my clothes. . . . I was working. . . . No! don't take that chair . . . it's dirty . . . That armchair there. . . . I'm very sorry, Madame Eliante."

She sat down and, with a serious look, very even, she looked around the room.

It was a room like any student room. Masses of books, a tapestry of books prevented one from contemplating the bareness of the walls, a few small knickknacks denoting youth and that *one moved in high society*.

Leon threw himself on the molded ear, letting slip a terrible piece of bloodless flesh. He covered the whole thing, ear and plaster, with a cloth, wiped his hands and brushed his jacket with a furious gesture.

Ah! He was a fine one, he was, for a love tryst.

And what about her!

Madame Donalger, still seated opposite the window, was now looking at the large frame of gray wood which framed in this room a superb painting by a master landscape artist, the treetops immobile at that moment under the sun like a painting under varnish.

She was dressed in an outfit of black wool, very sober, an astrakhan jacket thickened her waist, and her hair arranged in little flat bands, she wore a bonnet of black tulle, decorated with a plume of jet. She had an ivory complexion, yellower because of a little veil of black tulle, all smooth, which blocked her face with folds a hard as wrinkles.

She was not smiling, she was terrifying.

"I'm disturbing you, dear sir, for indeed, you weren't expecting me," she said, in an affectionate tone, without any bantering equivocation, in a very resigned tone, "but I made up my mind today, *in the fine weather*. If you only knew how one breathes outside? It smells almost of lilac, even though it's only March. Everything seems decided by the smell of the new flowers! And then you still didn't come. I have someone crying at home, that impels me towards you, despite the impropriety of my initiative. We must finish with it!"

Leon, standing in front of the fireplace, masking a very skimpy fire, a *widow's* fire, was wondering if she was going to continue, or if he should cut her off by bursting out laughing. But he was really in an intensely bad mood, poorly dressed, poorly combed, his hands were clammy, he had nothing but his fine youth left as any kind of excuse, and even then was it not an insult, in front of this woman so serious, so maternal?

"Someone crying at home, madam . . . I no longer grasp . . . "

Eliante, her hands meticulously gloved, stroked her little astrakhan muff, a muff which had the appearance of a shivery little animal, rolled into a ball.

"Does that surprise you, dear sir?"

"Yes, let's be clear: I have caused no pain, it has been caused me. I abstained . . . because . . . work . . . my exams."

He made a vague gesture indicating the books.

The famous fever was falling. He was no longer addressing Eliante. He was talking to a stranger, a woman instructed to report his words to her.

"Listen to me," she continued gently, "I know quite well that it's not your fault. It's fate, foreseen from all eternity. But a girl's love is always a very respectable thing, and one must do whatever possible to avoid complications. Missie loves you and told me so. Love at first sight! You surely realize that, if I take it upon myself to come and repeat it to you, it's because I hope for a good solution. You are free to withdraw, of course; however you don't have the right to avoid the customary explanations."

"Ah! Madam," bellowed Leon, clenching his fists, "I forbid you to touch my liberty, I alone am responsible for it. I'm listening to you because I'm polite, that's all!"

Eliante raised her eyelids.

Her eyes were as deep as chasms, without a glimmer. She must have been crying herself before coming there, but she would not shed a tear in front of him, one sensed it in the blackness of the look.

"Monsieur," she said coldly, "this is your house."

She could not have said more proudly: *this is my house*.

"Madam," murmured Leon turning his head away so as to no longer confront the presence of the stranger and hoping still in the sound of her voice, its inflections ordinarily so caressing, "I beg your pardon. I, too, have suffered, and I didn't go to you to air my troubles in your home, guessing that you would be inexorable. So, what do you want from me, now? Me, I'll not marry anyone, since I detest mystifications, and it seems to me simpler to declare that to you right away."

"Two betrayals . . . that's a lot for just one man who is still a child!" uttered Madame Donalger mockingly, with the ease of a society woman practicing the boldness of language mitigated by the accent.

"Two betrayals? You dumbfound me, dear madam."

"Well, we must clarify these questions and as the daylight of your fifth floor lends itself to it, we're going to throw them one after the other out onto your carpet."

She gave a heroic smile.

"Where they'll turn black from dust, I'm afraid," murmured the irascible Leon. "They forgot to sweep my rooms, this morning."

Ah! He had had a beautiful inspiration to lure her into what he thought to be an amorous trap.

He could have hit himself and would willingly have hit her.

"Missie," explained Eliante, "has taken to you not to juggle with, but to marry. It's very serious. She's even talking about *cohabitation*, a system of which these ladies recognize the usefulness, between the founding of two public nurseries. And since she claims that . . . I am pushing you away . . . I came to ask you if she really has any claims on . . . your affection, why you have forgotten the way to get to our house. We haven't run into you anywhere for a month now."

Leon went straight to the point.

"You admit then, madam, that someone juggled . . . "

"Yes, you with Missie."

"What? Me! That's too much! Madam, I have patience . . . but . . . "

He walked around his room rapidly and came and planted himself in front of the window panes, and drummed.

"Leon," declared Madame Donalger, dryly, serenely, "you told Missie that people don't marry forty-year-old women, but girls who resemble her, and she got permission to believe in a declaration. Your absence, involuntary or premeditated, added to the pain. From her head, it went down into her heart. That happens so fast in modern women! I, her adoptive mother, I don't intend to see her suffer uselessly. The first time she bebelieved in love, she didn't love. Today, it's different. I authorized her to write to you since she felt strengthened by your *permission*! She refused, she is . . . young and didn't dare, I think."

Leon had turned round gradually. At the last words, he leaped toward Eliante, stopped, his face convulsed.

"She lied, lied, lied," he cried, beside himself, losing all restraint, "yes, lied shamelessly, like the most shameless errand girl, you hear me! It's she who invented the story about *forty-year-olds*, it's she who tortured me horribly with her chambermaid's tales! And that, that's what you want me to marry? Are you mad, or do you want me to throw you out, all woman of the best society that you are? Do you think I don't suffer enough?"

And he too, because he was very young, scalding tears rose from his heart to his eyes.

Madame Donalger got up from her armchair, appearing paler than the palest ivory, and her pupils became phosphorescent.

"Would she have lied . . . that much?" she said musing aloud.

"Oh! Eliante," said Leon, sobbing into his closed fists and going to throw himself on his bed. "Oh! Eliante, what did you come here for, my God! *It's true then, that you are forty*? I love you so much, I do, in spite of everything."

The actress, or the woman, understood that she had played her part too well to cure him or cure herself, and that this time she had lost the game.

The age of a creature like Eliante was of little importance, in reality, but what was to count eternally, were the appearances it pleased her to assume.

She remained immobile, upright, solemn, without a movement of love. Not a muscle of her severe physiognomy moved, and her eyes were extinguished.

She was experienced, she knew that in the *costume of that role* she could do nothing either for him or for herself, that she would be ridiculous. And it was perhaps the most beautiful sacrifice that she offered the young man, this affected indifference, for Leon's despair could change into revolt and bring irreparable mockery.

What she wanted, above all, was to flee.

"Leon," she murmured gently, when he had calmed down a little, "Leon, my dear child, I really regret taking this step. Missie's wrongs are not serious. In a word, she has been jealous, and she has exaggerated. The memory which caresses an already distant phrase makes it sometimes more sonorous. Don't take a dislike to her. She is soured. Think of what she owes me. It's always so bitter to be in a state of dependence. . . . Don't come back . . . moreover, you're cured, that's the essential thing."

She headed for the door.

Leon Reille raised himself a little to see her leave.

"That's all," he stammered, "it's over already? You're leaving me on that note . . . and you believe in my cure, Madame Eliante?"

"Before answering you, sir, I must see Marie again, I must collect myself, I'm overwhelmed, because I feel myself in the presence of hatred."

"Not on my part, at least, surely?" he stammered, making himself very gentle, like a little boy who expects someone to wipe his face with a perfumed handkerchief.

She did not turn her head.

She felt a terrible desire to shout at him:

"Of course not, I can't give you the answer, I'm forty years old!"

And she thought:

"What's the use of denying it, since I look it, and moreover I will be in five years . . . a small thing for my love which dreams of eternity."

She died *a little* crossing the threshold of his door, but she took this formidable step courageously.

"Eliante!" cried Leon, hurrying after her.

She was already on the third floor when he leaned over the bannister.

He watched her descend, unable to guess the real reason for her fearful flight.

"She doesn't love me," he said going back in. "She's a businesswoman, who wants to marry her niece!"

He contemplated very painfully the extravagant little bonnet with silver bells, the cotillion accessory, which decorated the mirror over the fireplace.

"That's all I'll have left of her . . . and I still didn't get her to dance, take advantage of a waltz . . . like a man of the world."

His eyes fell, dejected.

They noticed, curled up in the corner of the fireplace, like a shivery little animal rolled into a ball, a black muff lined with white satin.

He let out a cry, the cry of an urchin who discovers a new toy.

She had forgotten her muff.

He sat down and brought it up onto his knees cautiously.

"Ah! my fellow! I've got you! It's clear it won't be to keep you here! In fact . . . she's going to come back . . . " (He rushed to the window and opened it.) "No . . . she's really left. The carriage, down there, is the coupé I know only too well! It's strange, she forgot something *of the décor*, in her life! . . . She loves me perhaps a little. . . . Just enough to make a muff for her pretty hands, a tiny corner of warmth. That damned statue of a lover! How stupid I was to cry in front of her. That won't happen to me a second time. . . . Without counting that she's going to go and tell it to that other goose, the *educated errand-girl*! If ever I meet her in a bedroom, that one, I. . . . Well, one thing's for sure, tomorrow, even though it's not *her day*, I'm returning the muff."

Eliante Donalger, meanwhile, was hurrying her driver:

"Faster, faster! I'm ill, Jean!"

She had, indeed, totally forgotten her muff, and yet it was because of that detail that the great passionate juggler had, at the moment of decisive choice, to abandon the present game in order to play the eternal one, by elevating her art to an apotheosis!

Eliante returned home via the garden of her house. She did not intend to encounter her niece, for she was suffering too much, and her niece would not have recognized her in the outfit of a devoted little widow returning from church.

She shut herself in her room, undressed, put on one of her favorite dresses again, a drapery of white velvet ruched with reddish lace. The dress of the Christmas engagement! She passed the voluptuousness of swan powder puffs over her face ravaged by sorrow and made herself beautiful once again with a new hope; but she was wounded in the chest, feeling her blood leaving her heart, which was beating fit to choke her.

When she had dreamed for an hour, her eyes closed, on a lounge chair, Eliante got up and rang.

"Have Mademoiselle Marie come down," she said to the maid who peeked through the doors.

Missie found, upon descending to her room, a calm woman, almost smiling.

"My dear girl, you exaggerated, and you put me, you put us, in a very false position both of us. I have just seen your fiancé. *He protests*."

Missie was rather pale, in an elegant outfit, shimmering with all the colors of the rainbow.

She began to cry, because everyone was crying, that day, except the main interested party.

She furiously bit her little handkerchief, not answering.

"Yes, I went to pay an ill-timed visit to this young man," said Eliante in a light tone, "my thirty-five years permit it, I think, and, if I'm not yet forty, I was able to figure out that

I've acquired that age, in the space of a day. That, really, quite sufficed to cure me of the boredom of ever being that age in front of your lovers."

"And what did you say to him?"

"But, the truth. I always tell the truth, even when juggling for little children who are sometimes men! I don't believe in hatred. I feel myself capable of intelligent cruelty, I don't know stupid or petty malice; so I walk calmly on dagger blades, it's my job. You called me a circus tumbler, one day, because I knew how to dance a Spanish step according to the sacred rituals, today you declare I'm forty, and you add things that someone had the delicacy not to repeat to me fortunately. I had to discover the crime. And what is more serious for you, for me, this young man doesn't love you, Missie. He may never love you."

Missie was standing, perplexed. The school teacher, strong with her liberated girl's new knowledge, sought an exposition of theories where the famous struggle for existence could get the upper hand again. It was the *errand girl* who triumphed. She remembered only the handsome young man whose discreet looks had conquered her. She forgot all philosophy, all spirit of revolt against the law of the strongest and, spontaneously repentant, she threw herself at the feet of Madame Donalger, sobbing for real.

"Oh! Eliante, forgive me," she cried in a broken tone, "forgive me! I didn't know the harm I was doing! *I thought he loved you or that you loved him*! So, I went mad with jealousy, and, with the help of the champagne, I said ridiculous things. No, Leon Reille had not promised to marry me, he told me, simply, that, if he pleased me, he considered that an honor. Me, well, I thought he preferred me or that he was courting me. He really did squeeze my arm very tight, and he smiled at me as he bent over my ear to tell me that white suited me better than other girls, because I had a warm complexion. In a word, since he left us, I see him all the time: his eyes, his mouth, his way of laughing, a little inside himself, and that great air of reserve he has, I thought: He is poor, too bad! We'll work, and you're so good, you would have given me a dowry just the same! Ah! don't tell me again, will you, that he's not coming back? The other one, I couldn't care less. But this one, he's stealing my heart."

"He's stealing her heart. . . . And my love? What are they doing to it both of them? Ah! he squeezed her arm hard! She's not lying any more now!" mused Eliante, her beautiful eyes staring at the ceiling of her room whence there fell on her a veil of shadows.

She smiled.

"Little one," she said in a dull voice, "I forgive you in the name of passion. You are suffering. Let's not talk about it any more. All is not yet lost. If he comes back this week, we'll try to repair our mistakes. If he hasn't come back by tomorrow, the god of love will judge between us! I myself shall go and fetch him."

The black Eros seemed to flash his emerald pupils at her.

Eliante took the young woman by the waist and kissed her.

"Oh! aunt," stammered Marie, almost pretty in a grand gesture of hope, "if you really wanted it, he'd come back . . . he'd come back, *if only for you*, and since, all the same, you cannot marry him, he'd end up marrying me, because I love him enough to try to correct my shortcomings."

"And if he forgot . . . to come back," questioned Eliante, whose beautiful impassive mask did not flinch.

"Then, we would leave France both of us, we'd go to those warm countries you miss, seek out the poor Ninaude to whom you were so attached, and whom my uncle sent back to Martinique to die."

"You have only today understood then that I was deeply

saddened by the departure of Ninaude, who wanted to die in my house, and whom you treated roughly because she was feeble?"

"Yes," breathed Marie, "I see now that, my Uncle Donalger and I, we must hurt you very often, for . . . we aren't your family. Ninaude, dirty and superstitious, was nevertheless much closer to you than me, Eliante; she loved you without disputing you, without seeking to understand you. Either one has to become your equal, or one must remain your slave. That makes people detest you . . . or love you too much."

Eliante, still impassive, closed her eyes.

Love, everywhere love! and she, the great actress, or the great victim of her own juggling, perhaps still did not know exactly what it was, humanly speaking. Vibrant and above the earth like a flaming torch consuming itself, she kept it all and yet dreamed of giving it all. She had the real knowledge, she had learned, to her cost, that love can spring from the source of the worst moral or physical pain, and she had wanted to drag through the mire the one who would become the elect! Why? With what right? For that obscure idea that *it would not last*? She had just taken the great desperate step, she had cried all her tears, during cruel nights in her mysterious bed, her bed of pleasure. She was made only to preach in the middle of the deserted temple, and tomorrow, if she became his mistress, she would be like the others, a very humble little errand girl trotting behind the triumphant master, and in exchange for her divine pride, she would not even bring happiness. She had the naiveté of Ninaude because she was from a land of dreams. She crossed herself gravely:

"It's my fault, it's my very great fault!" she thought, while Missie got up, sighing:

"Poor Ninaude! She really was dirty, all the same."

The next day, Leon Reille presented himself at Madame Donalger's. On the off chance, hoping to find her even though it was not her day, he had placed some tuberoses inside the muff, which he carried like a little cat, by its skin, with an awkward air, the air of someone who would very much like to throw an animal in the river.

Eliante was alone opposite the deaf diplomat, making him a complicated drink, one of those nun's recipes of which she possessed the secret. She was wearing, that day, a light-colored dress, an ample robe of floating mauve crepe, attached at the neck by an enormous amethyst. And she was beautiful with the beauty of a young wife who awaits the return of the husband.

The two men greeted each other ceremoniously.

"Oh! thank you, sir," said Eliante, frankly and simply moved, "I'm so happy to have forgotten it!"

"Perhaps I was wrong to come, madam? Isn't your brother-in-law going to imagine things . . . about the muff?" he added in a low voice.

"That's of no importance!" (She tapped her forehead gaily.) "The thing is there's a small formality to be taken care of. You're going to have to ask for someone in marriage . . . "

He was not listening to her at all, contemplating her silently, quite happy, he was, to rediscover her his *Eliante of love*.

"God!" he said finally, "you're beautiful today. It's beyond belief! But what shall I say about the muff . . . the one *belonging to the forty-year-old woman*?"

And he winked, half dazzled, half mocking.

"Uncle," cried Eliante at the top of her singing voice, "the gentleman, whom I went to see yesterday about you know what, is bringing me back my muff, and is coming to ask you, no doubt, permission to . . . come courting, for, after all, you are the head of the family."

Leon came out of his ecstasy, frowned.

"Eh? What is this new drawing-room juggling?"

"She naturally has told the same stories to her dear uncle," murmured Eliante, lowering her voice and shrugging her shoulders imperceptibly. "What do you expect, Leon, I can't do anything about it . . . we're the victims of fate . . . and since he's *formalistic*, he's capable of calling on you . . . to decide. Missie is out cycling. . . . When she returns . . . it will be necessary . . . unless she comes back with the whole gang, as usual!"

Leon Reille was a reserved man, a violent man, little used to worldly hypocrisy. He turned to the old man, who was drinking his aromatic drink while smoothing his side whiskers to give himself a dignified appearance and seeking to grasp some very diplomatic nuances.

"Monsieur Donalger," said Leon point-blank, "I'm here to pay court to Madame Eliante, and I hope that you will see no objection to it? She is free!"

Eliante burst out laughing. She would have watched the house blow up without displeasure that day. She felt free because she felt beautiful.

In front of a mirror, she slid the tuberoses into the helmet of her black hair, as a warrior's crest. Ah! it would be audacious, but it would be fair, since he loved her enough for that.

The dear uncle tugged his whiskers majestically, caressed his glass, his face anxious, following his fixed idea.

He replied, weighing his words, having heard nothing:

"Young man . . . I find you a bit . . . of a newcomer to our house, and, although your request honors me infinitely, I want to think about it. You are twenty-three years old, I believe, our little Marie is in no hurry on her side. On the other hand, I don't know your situation, but since you please my sister-in-law, I must admit to you that . . . you have a chance. . . . There remains the request of your family. I'm waiting for it. . . . Which Eliante will decide in the last resort. . . . We shall be sorry to be separated from Marie . . . as late as possible . . . "

And having got out of it with his honor, the old diplomat

beat a clever retreat. He took his glass, gave a little nod of benevolence.

"Come! Come! I shall leave you, you must have serious business to settle together. I long ago gave full power to Madame Donalger in matters concerning her niece."

When he had left, Leon, completely suffocated, raised his arms.

"The devil take it if I grasped what he meant, the old fool!"

Eliante was bursting with laughter. The creole, with a supple movement, threw herself onto the drawing-room carpet, where she leapt like a panther in gaiety.[1]

"Ah! it's so funny! Drama yesterday, vaudeville today! I knew, really I did, that one doesn't die of love nor of jealousy, on the contrary, one could be happy if one wanted to become simple, and it would be so good after having suffered. Leon, I can't help it, I'm bursting!"

"Would you like me to help you!" murmured Leon, vexed. "Only I don't understand, and this misunderstanding must not continue." (He added, his eyes troubled:) "I see only one way left." (He looked at her sitting at his feet, in the mauve flood of her dress, quite small, her knees folded against her chest, her arms crossed around her knees, her hands clasped and something terrifying in the depths of her pupils, something *green*, sparkling like the rays flashed by the black *Eros* in her bedroom.)

"Madame Eliante," he said, leaning over her shoulders, "it wouldn't be fair, neither for you nor her and, since someone must do something silly . . . it's normal it should be me. . . . What is your name . . . Madame Donalger . . . your . . . maiden name!"

Eliante stood up, more serious.

"Come here," she said, taking his wrists, and she led him to a piece of furniture, a large cupboard of red wood, at the other end of the drawing-room, "you, you want to see my birth certificate?"

"Yes," said Leon Reille brutally, "I want to know who you are, Madam Juggler? Well, husbands or lovers, that doesn't count for a lawyer . . . it's the maiden name which is always the *real* one."[2]

"Oh!" she sighed, "you men are cowards . . . you have no faith . . . the great faith which saves and moves mountains! You aren't concerned about knowing my real name . . . it's my age you want to verify legally."

Leon felt a chill in his heart.

She had guessed. He wanted equally some details about this mysterious woman who seemed to come to him from further away than . . . *solid ground*.

"So much the worse for you, Madam Juggler! You only had to not juggle to the bitter end, I want to kill the woman of yesterday so that she never returns."

"She will return in five years, Leon!"

"Five years! That's eternity in love."

"You think so?" sighed Eliante, painfully surprised.

She opened the red wood cupboard, looked there for a paper which she unfolded, a paper covered with a yellowed writing, all covered with stamps and giving off a peculiar smell of vetiver and island fruit.

Madame Donalger smoothed out this paper, placed it quite flat in the middle of the pedestal table where a large spray of white lilac was blooming.

The paper seemed yellower under the snowy flowers.

She put her index finger on one line.

"Born in 1862,[3] and since we are in 1897 . . . can you count?"

Bent over, Leon read attentively.

He had in front of him the proof that she had indeed told

the truth; curiously, that gave him the same chill in his heart as if he had confirmed the formidable forty years.

Then, brusquely, he shivered:

"Eh? What? . . . Blanche-Eliante, born of a legitimate father: *Charles-Edmond, Marquis de Massoubre.*[4] Ah! That's all we needed."

He took a step back pensively.

"That's what I was afraid of," he growled, forcing himself to be bantering, "you are the daughter of aristocrats, and, in my opinion, there are no opportunists worse than the toffs. They seem born to torture the poor world by their always hazardous expeditions. I, the son of their former scriveners, isn't it very fitting that I should remain the prey of their daughter?" (He added, darkly:) "Madam Marquise, the bride is decidedly too beautiful . . . *I'm not falling for it*, have to seduce me first, without that I'll never have the courage to give you my name."

She smiled sadly:

"How silly you are, little one, if you say what you think. Whoever I love is of my race."

"Yes . . . for the space of a kiss."

"Darling, that's called . . . an encounter."

"Hm! for dogs!"

Standing now, one in front of the other and looking each other up and down, their ripostes were flying in spite of them, as if they had picked up too nervously two old swords on the pretext of examining the rust on them. The parchment was between them, unfolded, keeping a sullen appearance, and it remained hostile to the one and to the other.

"Well, tell me then, you, the descendent of notaries," exclaimed Eliante hitting the table with her clenched fist, she so soft and so tempting, a moment ago, "you don't intend to make me atone for my ancestors? It's not a crime to be the daughter of a marquis, and, give me this credit, I had never mentioned it to you so as not to frighten you."

"And you acted well, madam, for I would never have set foot in your house again. Only, one could feel it! You like adventures too much and . . . the old races can only end badly."

"Churl!" cried Eliante, her pupils on fire.

"There!" said Leon Reille whose ears were burning in their turn. "It's starting! A sample of the day after our wedding!" (He crossed his arms like an irreverent student, very *marquis* in the manner of Voltaire, because the bourgeois from the provinces still read Voltaire.) "And I was going to ask you for her in marriage to settle things! Yes, a proud stupidity! I'm twenty-three years old, with a tender soul, no acceptable social position and . . . I would marry a daughter of the de Massoubre? Was he in the slave trade, your papa, my beautiful friend, that you absolutely insist on buying me like a slave, one minute to set me up with an errand girl, the next to have my skin legitimately? Yes, I'm a rustic, yes, I'm ferocious, but it's your fault, I suffered yesterday for a whole lifetime in hell, you hear? Now your turn, that's the rule. We're alone here, quite alone, aren't we? You'll only have me illegitimately at first, I tell you! We'll see afterwards! Keep that to yourself, I want to stay free. Enough ridiculous compromises! If I have the misfortune to love you, it's my only cerebral illness. I'm in fine form aside from my love. You'll spoil, by your own folly, my heart and my body as much as you please. As for my honor, my beauty, you won't touch it, no!"

Eliante, her eyelids suddenly closed, resumed her ivory mask.

"My dear child," she murmured, "we're exchanging big useless words. I want neither to marry you nor to treat you . . . as a slave, my entire conduct is there to prove it to you. I have no more need of you than you of me. I also love you, you seem to have forgotten it, but . . . maternally." (She gave a heroic smile.) "I meant: as a . . . noble mother, like yesterday! And really, if I had belonged to you a bit longer than the space of an engagement kiss, I think you would already be dead, I'm so . . . surprised by your upbringing. I think I hear Missie."

" . . . Already dead? That's a good joke! Another big word. So send me Monsieur Donalger's demands. With a pistol, one must be able to fight a deaf man, eh?"

Eliante replied gently.

"No need for my brother-in-law, my servants would be enough. They love me without question."

"You see," bellowed Leon Reille, getting completely carried away and throwing himself on her in a mad leap, "you put me on the level of your servants? Eliante, you're nothing but a . . . wretched woman!"

"You said it, sir."

There was a big silence.

Mademoiselle Marie Chamerot entered dressed in an ideal cycling outfit *for the modern fiancée*. Warned by her *dear uncle* that the handsome young man was there, she had proceeded to a toilette more befitting the occasion, that is to say that she had added primrose flowers to her bodice, in memory of the famous ball. She was wearing loose pants in white English wool, a white bolero over a white satin blouse cinched at the waist by a belt of white leather with a mother-of-pearl buckle, and on her disheveled head coquettishly, on the left, a jaunty little white felt hat decorated with a silk cord.

She walked like a baker's boy bringing the basket, the good basket filled with cakes for the rowdy children.

Leon, red with anger, turned to her and got this bowl of milk full in the face.

He was showered, fortunately, at the moment he was going mad.

"Mademoiselle!" he said, bowing very low, a little confused by his disordered gestures with regard to Eliante.

"Sir!" said Marie Chamerot, terrorized by the idea that her aunt could humiliate her in front of him.

And she modestly contemplated her bicycling shoes, shoes too large, of white skin.

Was her fate finally going to be decided?

The daughter of the Marquis de Massoubre took her hands affectionately.

"You're charming, Marie, ever since you became a bit more womanly! Don't torment yourself about the future. If the gentleman isn't yet your official fiancé . . . he has received permission to court . . . he'll do it, he's a gallant man I can answer for, since . . . he owes it to me to merit my confidence. Don't offend each other with useless proposals, and when love comes to you, the great love which is always very noble, don't scare it away with speeches; love seldom likes phrases. Don't hesitate to take advantage of your beautiful youth; me, I'm for the crossing of new races . . . happiness . . . that never waits."

Eliante was smiling, perfectly calm.

Missie burst out sobbing, since a great joy always overflows in tears. Leon, in despair, startled, watched her cry. He would have preferred a duel.

"Oh! aunt, my good dear aunt? . . . You really want me to marry him?"

"Actresses don't come any better!" growled Leon between his enraged teeth.

Eliante removes the last branch of tuberoses remaining in her hair.

"Here, my little girl, the flowers of illusion, try to keep them a bit longer than I did and don't forget that love goes before pride in real women." (She turned to Leon.) "Aren't I pretty as a noble mother? . . . Goodbye, sir."

And she ran away, for she was suffocating.

The young people contemplated each other, sadly embarrassed.

"Mademoiselle," began Leon hoarsely, "I have just offended your aunt, and she's right to punish me; however, the punishment must not affect you, you're beyond, this time, all these worldly complications. Go and find Madame Donalger quickly, I beg you, calm her down! and let's try to explain ourselves better the three of us. I've never thought to ask either for her hand or yours. I wouldn't dare. All that, it's a never-ending comedy! Go and find her, I beg you."

"I understand fully, sir! You still love her?"

She maintained a soft, resigned little expression. She let out a deep sigh, examined once again her cycling shoes.

"I'll wait . . . since I'm *smitten*, too."

Leon could not help laughing, while she dabbed her tears with a naive gesture.

"Come on, Missie," he said very quietly, "you're exaggerating, and everyone exaggerates in this house. Marie, you do me a harm, no an honor that I don't deserve! Think, I can't marry you, I've already told you that I possess neither fortune nor position. It would be necessary at least to wait until my parents . . . "

"We'll wait!" sighed Marie, whose pride was not her main shortcoming.

And they both sat down at opposite ends of a couch, putting their chins on their palms. Then, mechanically, seeing that Eliante was not coming back, they each lit a cigarette:

"Would you care for a light?" asked Leon politely.

"Willingly!" replied Marie.

. . . Because, in students or in errand girls, bad habits are above all circumstances.

CHAPTER TEN

"MY beloved,

"The love letter *which must fall into the water*, it is one of my manias, you see, and I'm writing to you because women write at certain turning points in their existence like they cry, without knowing why. Besides, I never cry in front of someone, and when I write . . . it is in order to be alone!

"You are very kind both of you to have insisted, the other day. While you were knocking on my door, I was in the process of picking up the pieces of my black Eros, the little marble statue which collapsed in my room—perhaps I must have pushed it without noticing—and it smashed.

"Faithful to my philosophy of fatalistic creole who knows that a statue, or a slave, can be found again, I threw the remains of it to one side, and I am trying to not think about it any more.

"But I am thinking about you, I am thinking about you.[1] Good Lord, how late it was when you came to my door! What on earth were you doing?

" . . . Yes, you came very late to my house, my poor empty house, sir and dear lover! Just think that I had been waiting since dawn, my body bent out of the window, looking hard at those who came, those who went, saying to myself with each new passerby: 'That's not him, for he doesn't have the wings of Eros, I don't know him, me, the priestess of Eros he hasn't given me the mysterious sign!' And evening came after the young men, the passersby thinned out, a bitter smell came up from the valley, right up to me, the smell of green spaces that curl up and give up their soul in the agony of the day, the dusk enveloped the hills with a veil of blue . . . violet . . . black . . . the night!

"So, as the first star came out like the eye of Eros, soft and cruel, with a moonlight which pierces, you finally arrived, walking in the direction of my house quite by chance. Whether it was the glow of the star or my fatigue with living in a house which was filling up with shadows, I thought that I had seen the envoy of Eros, the envoy of God! You were raising your head to my window and you had made the sign.

"I went downstairs like a madwoman . . . but not fast enough. Lazy and still coiled up like a snake in the warmth of the temples, I amused myself by making the pearls of my dress click and by shaking my scarf so that the noise of the jewels, the intoxicating scent of the perfumes, should let you know who I was before showing you the whiteness of my arms.

"Quite mad is the woman who amuses herself with her beauty before laying her body at the knees of her master!

"Outside, it was nighttime. I could no longer find you. You had crossed the threshold of my house, however; but, unable to see clearly, its shadow had seemed formidable to you, full of ambushes, and you had left.

"I ran . . . I went madly right into the middle of the road, and I met another man, almost your brother, who said to me: 'Are you really looking for someone?' 'I'm looking for the love of my life or the life of my love,' I answered. 'I know it's necessary to wait a lot to be happy. I would never dare to give myself to the first one I met for fear it not be *him.* If I make a mistake by taking you home, would I not be obliged to kill you so that Eros should receive your blood in reparation for the injury done to his priestess! What I respect the most in myself is my god!' 'Woman,' he said laughing, 'we don't speak the same language, as for me, I don't have time to linger over these trifles which attach or exasperate with no profit for human joy!' 'But,' I added timidly, 'perhaps I'll teach you divine joy!' I saw clearly, in the way he got angry, that indeed we were not speaking the same language. I was mad. He was reasonable.

"That made two different races.

"And I returned home slowly, where I remained alone, having always been alone, despite my beauty, but much more alone now, for I felt that the envoy of Eros would no longer pass in front of my dark house.

"It was too late!

" . . . Come along! Do not read that seriously! I am no longer crying, am I, I am writing love letters *which fall into the water*. You know full well, my dear little friend? So do what you want with your life, you are free, and come and see us from time to time, girls who hope must not be left to grow sad. Marie will perhaps do like me, she will console herself.

"I no longer hold your hard words against you. Have I not said worse things? They came out of our inner depths, and it is the voice of our fathers that spoke them, in spite of our loving lips! You wanted very sincerely to marry me, to *regularize* love. . . . You spoke for three minutes like a notary checking dates and ascertaining the authenticity of the titles, and I, who have never much known my family, I had the reaction of the light Marquis de Massoubre, with the heavy name, always ready, it seems, to pick a quarrel with people.

"And from that our beautiful love died. (I mean: *the antique Eros*.)

"I beg you to come and see us . . .

"Do not answer me anything cruel. Me, I am quite comfortable being a beggar of love . . . since I am not your mistress. So I have every right, and *my father* can forbid me nothing, in a loud voice, in the inner depths of my heart. I do not give a hoot about my respected father, for I too am the Marquis de Massoubre, and *alone*, today, I am responsible for

Eliante Donalger"

"P.S.—By the way: do not bring my letters back under pretext of . . . propriety, I have never been able to take back that which I have once given freely."

E.D.

(Telegram)

"Ah! I can breathe! I will go to see you, my Eliante. Bring your letters back? I had thought of it, but I will return them to you when you become my wife, and, I shall wait five years to marry you. I shall be the hero, not having been able to be the man, if there really is heroism in marrying on the same day all the women in love in one madwoman; we shall see who proves to be the more of a *marquis*! If I am not noble, I am very stubborn, and stubbornness, it is the nobility of notaries, of that of doctors."

Leon Reille.

"P.S.—Missie disgusts me as much as poached eggs in cream."

L.R.

CHAPTER ELEVEN

(By telegram, the next day.)

"Tonight . . . "

Eliante Donalger.

CHAPTER TWELVE

HE entered, that spring day, as on Christmas day, via the little garden the gate of which was open.

His heart was beating deliciously, and he felt an irreverent gaiety, without having, however, the ridiculous ideas of a man conceited by imminent triumph.

She was giving in.

That was simpler, more in keeping with life; but that would not happen on its own, for a juggler of her calibre was bound to contrive some surprises for him.

Pleasant or unpleasant, the surprises? Would he be obliged to get angry at the last minute, to act like the trainers confronted with the *air drinker*, the famous mare whose eyes had to be burned to make her carry Mohammed?

And he recapitulated:

"No, she won't kill herself, but she's capable of trying, all the same? She will have sent Missie to the public nurseries and the deaf diplomat to his friend the wine taster. We'll have plenty of time to discuss the type of death, in the afternoon. Toward evening, a light meal, wine from the islands, will soften us up. Me, I demand asphyxiation by roses. I've sent enough of them to decorate her entire room and to scatter on the carpets. Now, there's poison and a bullet from a revolver. Very dirty in its results, poison; the revolver . . . that's quite old hat, moreover, that makes a lot of noise, especially when one misses, and that sets the servants onto you. It remains to persuade her that by keeping her in bed, for a week, I undertake to make her forget the taste of Chinese pimento with which Monsieur Donalger used to season his conjugal caresses. I believe, all things considered, that my most dangerous enemy is that naval officer who still commands the phantom vessel of her dreams. There are some people who must be buried under mountains! It's funny, I feel well disposed, very happy, I'm no longer afraid of her, but, *the dead man* obsesses me. I'd better shake that off smartly. After all, yesterday, I saw her as a magician capable of casting a spell on me; today, I have the glorious awakening of the spectator who returns to the theatre to find the great actress at his sides, in flesh and blood, but not too much bone, offering her arms, minus the plaster. The husband? The prompter, of course! I have no need to trouble myself about my own lines. To begin with, we won't talk any more. The eternal things have been said! . . . Confound it! . . . Missie!"

Standing, on the front steps, Marie Chamerot greeted him, blushing a little, charming moreover, for she was growing more beautiful since being sincerely taken by the student. She too was trying to smother in her heart the furious beating of Eros's wings! Her eyes were shining, adding hidden meanings to the slightest phrases; her hair was done like a warrior of love like her aunt, she proudly wore the smooth helmet of her hair, revealing her forehead, showing her nape, and she had put on again, that day, a coquettish April outfit of white and pink, little Pompadour bouquets drowning in a cream background. Ever the poached eggs in cream! and already the gallant tip of the carmine bud which bursts its envelope.

"Hello, mademoiselle! You're not cycling today then? Is Madame Donalger well? Am I arriving too early? You were on your way out? I'm so badly brought up."

"No, sir, we weren't about to go out. My aunt is a little poorly."

"What's the matter with her?" interrupted the anxious young man, all his triumphant gaiety having flown away.

"Oh! nothing serious! She got up very late, complained of nervous pains, lunched better than usual however; she drank some wine, she who never drinks any, and she went down to her apartments, telling me she wanted to prepare her room to show us her beautiful robes. You know, the collection from the hot countries? On the contrary, she is very gay, although ailing, she wants to make us dance . . . to teach you, sir."

And she sketched a gracious bow.

"She isn't seriously ill, Marie, you would tell me, wouldn't you?"

Marie examined the young man, with a worried expression, as if she were seeing him for the first time. Her gaze of a small free person had something hard, a startled fear or a resolution, mixed with an inexplicable timidity.

"I'll learn, mademoiselle, I'll learn anything she wants, and I hope you'll help me?" murmured Leon politely.

"Oh! me, I don't know the Spanish rituals! It will be very entertaining for you if she gets involved in it. Me, I'm still a pupil."

"A very . . . well-trained pupil, mademoiselle! I've seen you dance." (They returned together to the water-green dining room.) "My highest compliments on your dress, Missie, and on your new hairstyle? A waist, hair! You're exquisite! Do you mind?"

And he took a flower from her corsage, a little half-opened bud, which he slipped into his buttonhole.

"It's not fair!" she said sadly, "You don't love me . . . "

"You think I don't love you? You're mistaken, mademoiselle. Today, the effect of spring, I love everyone, I love all women . . . and I would marry them all if someone wanted to give me them all! Alas, no one ever gives me anything . . . except flowers . . . and even then, only when I . . . take them back?"

"Excuse me! When you steal them!" retorted Missie with fire in her cheeks, not knowing that the young man had sent bunches of roses to her aunt, that very morning.

"God!" said the student hypocritically, "one takes ones goods where one finds them! there's an ambiguity there, but it doesn't concern you. Missie, show me your progress in the art of medicine, eh! in what way do you look after Madame Donalger's migraines, my dear colleague?"

"You insist that I talk to you about her? Do you want me to go and fetch her? She's getting dressed. You are incorrigible, sir. You're the one who won't be cured easily. I don't look after my aunt. She's afraid of all the doctors, including student doctors, you know!"

"Bah! Am I so terrible then, mademoiselle my dear colleague?"

He threw his hat and his cane onto a couch with the gesture of a man who is at home. Mademoiselle Chamerot was smiling, but he noticed that her eyes were all humid from a deep emotion. There was cruelty in making fun of her on such a day. Since Madame Donalger would be appearing, he would be good, tender, brotherly. He would do his job of seducer, discreetly, while waiting for something better.

"I beg you, Missie," he said very winningly, planting himself in front of her and offering his hands, "if she cannot bear me, try to make me forget it for one afternoon. Be charitable?"

"Yet it's true," sighed Missie, squeezing his hands despite

her violent desire to turn her back on him, "I must love you for those who don't love you. She couldn't care less, about lovers, could she?"

Leon shook his head, smiling.

"She's wrong . . . a nice warm heart, that's a very pleasant thing to place on the corner of the mantelpiece when one is reading novels."

Marie shrugged her shoulders, and unable to hold back any longer, she cried, in her purest Parisian ragamuffin voice:

"Your heart? Fine! She has a cupboard full of them, warm hearts. And she doesn't use them, it's like her beautiful robes that mildew! I tell you she's mad!"

"That's my opinion absolutely!" declared Leon, who could not help laughing and pulling her up to him to kiss her chastely, on the forehead.

Marie let go of his hands, and went to arrange some fruit on a crystal fruit stand.

"We'll have a light meal with her," she said feverishly, trying to disguise her emotion; "Mademoiselle Louise will take part; we'll eat frangipani tartlets, we'll drink cream of violets, and we'll taste the Anam apples which are ripe, apparently! Are you familiar with Anam apples? You suck them with straws, like sorbet. It's very good. Mademoiselle Louise, that's the musician from the white ball, a tall blond, more blond than me; she wears her hair in virgin's bandeaux and, if she didn't have such a long nose, she'd be quite beautiful; but, there you are, I've noticed that all the musicians had long noses!"

"Enough about the Anam apples! My appetite is whetted, and there will never be enough of it," affirmed the young man; "only what is Mademoiselle Louise's nose doing in this fine dessert, my dear Missie?"

"You're funny! We can't teach you to dance without her.

Mademoiselle Frehel will take the piano. My aunt doesn't allow us to make our own music, so long as there are great artists to take care of it."

"I recognize her well in that! Damned princess!" he growled, but he kept his thoughts to himself. Eliante's voice was heard, behind the door, Eliante's voice, her real voice.

She entered, leading Mademoiselle Louise Frehel by the arm.

"Hello, children" said Eliante affectionately, her eyes half closed like someone who has just woken up, "I bring you our Madonna of the harp, she is most kind to have put herself out for us. Mademoiselle Louise, may I introduce Monsieur Leon Reille, a future dancer . . . if he wants to learn, and he must learn. You are well, my dear friend. Me, I'm nervous . . . I'll break everything . . . my fingers are trembling. . . . Look!"

She held her hand out to him.

Leon felt inundated by a powerful joy. She was there, standing, smiling, and if her small hand was trembling, she had her beautiful eyes of love, her most passionate eyes, and, if she did not yet dare to show them to others, he sensed them clearly beneath their fringe of fur. She was in white, draped with a large ivory velvet; she was wearing the engagement dress, the Christmas dress.

"Christmas!" answered the young man's heart with a leap.

"Madam, in your school," he said bowing, "what wouldn't one learn? And how is Monsieur Donalger?"

"My brother-in-law is at a lawyer's, at the moment, a matter of paperwork for which I cannot take responsibility myself. I think we'll see him either for our collation, or for dinner, for we'll keep you this evening, Monsieur Reille, we shan't dismiss you until after dark. The question is settled."

"I understand perfectly well," said the young man to himself reassured, "I'll pretend to leave *officially*, and I'll come back through the garden, once the lights go out; there's no longer any question of suicide, and that simplifies the outcome. This is a wedding night which promises to be even better than I dared dream. I almost feel like learning to dance."

Missie fell upon the neck of the tall blond girl. The latter removed her hat, her coat, and appeared artistically dressed in a brown wool dress, a sort of nun's outfit with an austere grace, making the virginal bandeaux and aquiline nose stand out . . . yes, a little long, but prettily shaped, something of a virtuoso.

And the three women, preceding the young man, entered the temple.

The high chamber was lit by its three oval windows all gleaming with sun; the three topazes were streaming with magnificent fires without the slightest indication of landscape and bathed in a warm light all the dark furniture; Leon recognized, in the place of the antique Eros, his roses from the morning, soaking in a colossal bowl of Venetian glass, with nuances of opal. Above the swan tuffet, flowers of every color intertwined, mingled, rebelled, little buds or large blooming roses, like cupids in a nest, and they overflowed onto the white fur, they fell everywhere. Petals flew in all directions, but this clear and scented cascade could not compete with the violence of the perfume of the mysterious room. It smelled of vetiver, also island fruit . . . and higher up, beneath the vault of darkness, there reigned that inexplicable smell of *negro oil*, of which Madame Donalger sometimes spoke, a wild animal smell.

Fast asleep, the lions, the tigers, the panthers presented still their formidable heads in the middle of panels of gold cloth and still the unusual big bed, in the shape of an egg, all pale under the peacock blue Brousse silks, seemed protected by them like the egg of the world, the seed of all love.

The three women began to chatter quietly.

"You've hidden the piano? That's just like you! Poor piano! you treat it with disdain, madam," Mademoiselle Louise Frehel was saying while opening a keyboard in the middle of a little alcove of green palms.

And the piano-monster showed its white teeth, brutally. It had the air of a giant negro who smelled thus of rancid oil, yawning.

"Oh! aunt, our Anam apples! They're much too soft!" declared Missie, busying herself with a pretty lacquer table with several levels, all piled high with special and delicate dishes.

"Well, we'll have to squeeze them in the ice pail," answered Madame Donalger, very frightened merely at the idea that they would not be edible.

And the two women, during a tender waltz prelude, knelt before a silver pail filled with ice, plunged their agile hands, withdrew round and sonorous silver utensils, knocking against each other with strange cymbal noises, placed the fruit there gently, as one would put the heads of little children on cushions in their cribs.

Leon was smiling. He was king, that spring day, and it was his male royalty that the three adorable women were cradling.

"Tonight!" he was thinking.

Never did any young groom have a more marvelous wedding day, and never again would he see that. Everything which made the beauty of life was uniting to please him and prepare his happiness.

When Eliante stood up again, leaving to Missie the task of powdering with crushed ice her little silver molds in which lay the Anam apples, their eyes met.

He nervously bit his lips.

Very serious, Eliante advanced toward him, rounded her arm above her head, as though suddenly carrying a lyre.

"Now," she said, "we must amuse ourselves without remembering that life . . . passes."

"I love you," answered Leon his voice all trembling with hope, "and it will never pass fast enough, today."

"Missie," called Madame Donalger closing her eyes, "your minuet, if you please, that will give a first lesson in deportment to our pupil."

Mademoiselle Louise Frehel began the minuet in a rapt silence. Eliante came to lean on the piano. Leon sat on the swan tuffet, and Missie, all bathed in blond light, stood up almost pretty, with the prettiness of an engraving in the topaz depths of the room.

There was there a wide green cloth spread out on the Smyrna carpet, forming a close-cropped lawn, and she seemed to dance on the grass of a park, in the setting sun. Missie, a bit thin, a bit hip-shot, walking like a baker's boy who cycles with a basket, became suddenly elegant, posed, and the charm of the bittersweet melody, fragile, slightly sharp, helping, she made a solemn curtsey, together with a puckering of the mouth and eyelids of the most comic effect.

The minuet picked up speed, her lively feet stepping out of step, she arrived too soon on the last chord, executed a slide, two or three jumps of a goat in revolt, and landed on a bow, brief and bold, of her own invention.

Leon broke out in warm applause.

"Bravo! . . . it's wonderful, totally successful, but I quite hope that no one is going to ask me to do as much. . . . I would just as soon go hang myself!"

"No one's asking you to learn that, it's too difficult," generously declared Missie out of breath and fanning herself with her handkerchief, "Mademoiselle Frehel is now going to dance a pavane for us. She's very clever, you know, and I shall accompany her. It's only to train your sight. You understand, old friend!"

"Me, I'm the happiest of the four, if no one makes me do anything. I'll understand, on condition I remain seated."

"Your turn will come, sir," said Mademoiselle Frehel in passing, with a kind smile of encouragement, for she found him pleasing, this handsome wild boy, who snuggled up in their skirts with the sly joy of a great voluptuous cat.

And Missie played the pavane. And Eliante went to look for a fan for the dancer. Curiously, this virgin on the harp in the homespun outfit immediately took on the attitudes of a grand lady of the great century. She shook her skirt to one side and her fan to the other, as if she would make brocade and a scepter slide between her fingers. Her gentle, cadenced movements, always noble, had an extraordinary harmony. Leon, this time, was no longer laughing, he was beginning to realize that dance is probably not what shallow people think . . . in the Latin Quarter.

"Oh! how beautiful! What purity of line! More! More! Mademoiselle! One would think oneself in the galleries of Versailles."

"You should see her dance in court costume," said Eliante who was daydreaming behind him, her forehead pressed against the freshness of the bowl filled with roses.

"No! I prefer her nun's dress, it's more mysterious, and the nobility of her art is more transparent in it."

Eliante let her moist hand fall on the young man's shoulder.

"Is it not the case," she said quite quietly, "that art can be a consolation for many things. . . . That girl there is very poor, very good, still very pure, and no one dreams of marrying her, I think she suffers from it."

"Yes," said Leon, touching his nose with his index finger, "*it's too long*!"

A haughty smile pulled back Madame Donalger's lips.

"You talk like Missie. She's beautiful, that girl."

"If you say so," breathed the young man, taking advantage of Missie's presence at the piano to rub his head against

Eliante's bodice. The latter pulled away, a flash of lightning in her pupils.

Yet there was a storm brewing in this atmosphere of love, of ferocious jealousies which were sleeping like great beasts hung and crucified on the walls, and, sometimes, in a waft of the fan scattering the odor of the flowers and the savor of island fruit, one could smell rising above it the perfume of negro races, of cannibals!

After the pavane, Missie and Leon danced, argued, shouted themselves hoarse and ended up grabbing hold of each other. It was because of the waltz.

Mademoiselle Frehel struck desperate chords, in an effort to inculcate the science of rhythm in the young man who was getting irritated little by little.

At one point, Missie threatened to pinch him.

So, he came, quite piteous, toward Eliante.

"Wouldn't you like to take charge of me?"

"No," she said in a hard voice. "I can only dance with those who already know how. I'm too old to learn . . . how to not know."

"Cruel woman! You're hatefully cruel! Let's try . . . "

"Let's eat first, we'll dance later," said Eliante escaping from his arms.

She pushed the table into the middle of the room.

"Wait a minute . . . " thought Leon, "something's wrong . . . but what? Modesty? Remorse? The idea of getting revenge for her defeat by a new bout of coquetry? I've got her and I'll have her . . . this nervous beauty . . . or tonight's the night I'll beat her!"

The wild cat was beginning to try its claws on the white furs.

He came and sat on the right of Eliante, and Mademoiselle Frehel placed herself on the left, Missie opposite.

There was a fine clinking of little spoons on porcelain and

crystal, lively words falling in swipes on the fruit and greedy bites in the tasty pulps. The Anam apples were a big success. Missie and Leon changed straws without noticing. Leon was quickly becoming intoxicated, for he could feel Eliante's knee near his. Lightly stroke her knee? That night he would have all of her! It cost him little to be respectful. Missie, in passing him a glass of champagne, spilled some on the tablecloth, and Mademoiselle Frehel said gaily:

"Sign of a wedding!"

"A promise of love, mademoiselle!" answered Leon sharply.

"It's more modest," ventured Marie, and the two girls broke out laughing while drinking to his health.

Leon was looking at Eliante. She was not laughing. An infinite suffering occasionally contracted her beautiful face, decomposed it into a tragic mask, she seemed one minute absent, in a completely different world, then she bent over her guests, cut up the cakes, served the creams and peeled fruit for them. Had she then given all her love and did she have none left to make her quiver with impatience with him?

After the meal, servants took away the table and, furtively, brought back two huge chests. A curiosity inflamed Leon and the girls. It was the oriental costumes.

The large chests of camphor wood, studded with copper, seemed to have crossed the seas quite often. . . . One of them, mildewed, its nails rusty, retained a sort of humidity as though emerging from a shipwreck.

Eliante opened the chests and the girls let out cries of admiration, while the young man, with the awkward satisfaction of a ravaging animal, pulled to himself velvets, silks, multicolored wools spangled with gold and silver, with glass trinkets, with fringes, with decorations of shell or of human teeth. All this, the simple necklaces, the slightly muddy scarves, the headgear with sequins and the gauze veils dotted with colored pearls, these were the joys of love stolen from women or altered for one woman. Eliante had worn all that; and his hands becoming feverish, he plunged them sensuously into this torrent of sweet things which caressed his palms. There were skirts of heavy wool and pants of filigreed damask, blouses of silk light as clouds, enormous belts, inlaid and studded with gems. The girls' ecstasy knew no bounds. Missie's eyes were popping out of her head, and the Madonna, Mademoiselle Frehel, losing her artist's seriousness, was sitting on the floor so as to better handle and size up the embroideries.

"Come along, young ladies, unfold the screens and get dressed up. You must try on my robes."

It was complete delirium. The joyful gamine and the serious Madonna rushed, the former to a brilliant gold and blue Turkish outfit, the latter to an ample Japanese robe with silver floral patterns on a green background. Behind the screens, one could hear the metal hooks clicking and the satins brushing against each other. An odor of fresh coquette mixed with the last sugary vapors of the meal.

But above that, far above emerged the strong smell of pepper exhaled by the open chests, a smell of piracy.

Soon Leon had around him, fluttering, whirling, stopping in front of the mirrors or consulting his taste, all the beauties of a harem; the two girls changed costume four times, then returned to the Turkish lady and the Japanese lady who suited them better. Completely pale, completely white, kneeling in front of the chests, ceaselessly plunging her arms in and pulling out her loaded beautiful hands, Madame Donalger was still drawing out new riches. She pulled out a Malaysian costume, a *sarong* of rough green wool, decorated with black pearls, a scarf of black and yellow material, sounding beneath her nail like dry leaves, and a hat of old straw all full of saffron powder. On the hat hung a terrible madras kerchief, and to the scarf was attached, in a leather sheath, a *kriss* with a blade bent like a sinister reptilian sting, then an *oceanian* costume, very scant, a narrow pagne with blue stripes on white cotton, a little case of carved bone containing a set of fish bone pins. Those . . . one could hardly try out.

"There! that's all! My young friends, I'm giving them to you," declared Eliante in a slow voice. "Share them as sisters. Each of you take a chest to put them in, where they will keep perhaps for a few years, but I notice that these materials smell of mildew. They're getting old, I don't want to keep them here any more. Toys are made to amuse children."

Missie let out a cry. Mademoiselle Frehel joined her hands:

"Oh! Madame, what an idea! Why sacrifice them to us when you're still going to the ball? That must be a gold mine for the fancy dress season."

"I'm not going to the ball again," said Madame Donalger, " . . . at least this winter," she added in a darker tone.

Leon smiled proudly.

"The laurels have been cut down,"[1] he murmured, with a gesture which cut across Eliante's fingers in the process of unfolding a great veil of gauze riddled with pearls.

Missie and Mademoiselle Frehel moved off a little, whispering. He understood. Certainly she had obeyed her summons. She was dividing her fortune between her niece and her brother-in-law, which brother-in-law had gone to his lawyer that very day for some *matter of paperwork*, and, now, she was distributing the souvenirs of her conjugal life to the two girls. It was good, it was fine! He felt mad. . . . Afterward, they would run away together to love one another!

And on his knees in the silks, completely black, very supple, dressed in his simple student's jacket, a little rose in his buttonhole, his young head pale with pleasure raised toward her, all proud of his role as exterminating demon, his eyes sparkling from the reflection of the stones, Leon Reille crawled up to her:

"Shall I not see you dance for me alone? Will you not dress up also for me to admire you? Why do you perpetually efface yourself in front of me when my eyes seek you out? You don't love me any more then, Eliante."

He was begging like a jealous child, wanting his share of the toys.

"You demand it?"

"Yes, I want it! I want you to be the most beautiful here, the youngest, and she whom I must prefer. If you don't obey me absolutely, I'll beat you, tonight, I'll become the meanest of men!"

Eliante replied:

"You're right! I've kept two outfits. I'll put them on . . . when it's time . . . "

Mademoiselle Frehel, at the piano, began a waltz.

Missie came to invite *her fiancé*. They waltzed very badly, arguing, then it was the Japanese lady's turn, but that did not go any better than with the Turkish lady. Eliante smiled.

Leon in spite, threw himself on the ground, shouting:

"No, it's no use, I'll never learn. Moreover man isn't made to dance, he looks stupid. I resign, ladies."

"He's right," said Eliante solemnly, stopping with a sign the two girls, who were whipping him with a scarf; "dance, which is the very expression of the grace of love, cannot concern man. Inevitably a man must watch dancing . . . then throw in his handkerchief."

"That's it," cried Leon enthusiastically! "Quick, ladies, spread out the mats, bring the cushions, fan me, for I'm very warm, then let my hookah be prepared, no, my cigarettes, which Mademoiselle Missie still has in her pocket and . . . I'm the king, I'm resting."

Submissively, the girls spread out burnous, shawls and scarves, piled up cushions, and he was presented with cigarettes on a tray, while Louise Frehel swayed in harmonious movements a huge multicolored fan.

"That's better, much better," declared Leon, stretching out on the softness of the silks opposite a big dead tiger. "What a comfortable existence! Now, I permit you to dance before me. I'll distribute rewards. Whose turn is it, ladies?"

"It's Madame Eliante's turn, if she isn't too tired," said Louise Frehel smoothing the Madonna's bandeaux. "We must ask for her *iota*, if she deigns . . . it's unheard of. Would you mind, madam, just for the three of us, within the family."

"Excuse me," interrupted Leon peremptorily, "for me alone, if you please. Let's not forget that I'm the king."

Missie begged:

"Oh! dear aunt, since uncle hasn't returned, he won't scold you."

"Yes, yes," answered the distant voice of Eliante, "I'm getting dressed."

Between two puffs of cigarette, Leon had time to pinch Missie's ankle and to kiss in passing a white arm which might well have belonged to Louise Frehel. Missie pulled his hair by the handful, and Louise blushed slightly.

"You understand, my dear little things," replied the student completely intoxicated because the smoke, the peppery smells of the fabrics and the fumes of the champagne were combining terribly in his brain, "since I'm the king, you're my slaves . . . and I forbid you to shout!"

As well brought-up girls, they did not shout, very obliging toward this handsome boy all quivering with pleasure and who, moreover, was thinking of another as he caressed them . . .

"Mademoiselle Louise," said a muffled voice behind a screen, "would you go to the piano, I'm ready; and you, Missie, arrange some light. Evening's falling, and one can no longer see in my room."

With a leap, Mademoiselle Frehel was in her place, and with another leap Missie went to press an electric button.

The room was set ablaze. The smoke, the fumes seemed to go back up to the ceiling, under the black vault, in light wreaths. On the panels of gold cloth, the wild animals polished their silky fur, the lacquer furniture threw off flares of bluish stars, and the big Venetian bowl full of roses, in the middle of the temple, set up the simple grace of life in the innocent and blessed person of the flower.

"They're well trained, the girls!" thought Leon, smoking, his forehead in the clouds. "Ah, the temple's being lit up! If Madame Eliante could blaze a little . . . that would be something else."

Then it sounded like the thunder of a storm, the dull and hammering sound of the tambourines that Mademoiselle Frehel, who made the piano-monster into everything she wanted, imitated to a marvel, then like the grinding of mandolins, tuning up or clashing with each other.

The screen parted.

"Eh, Spain!" cried Leon, raising himself on one elbow, and putting his hand above his eyes to protect them.

"Olé! Olé!" replied the girls in echo.

And the thundering of the Spanish dance accelerated, humming and violent with notes, vibrating suddenly, in a burst of splintering crystal.

In the cold daylight of the electricity, on the smooth green cloth, having as sole decoration a topaz sun, a woman appeared dressed in a skirt of yellow satin, midlength and almost clinging, a skirt without the traditional underskirts of the theatre. One sensed that the woman was wretched and could not offer herself, nor offer the luxury of laces. The dress was covered with a high flounce of black chenille forming a net. A toreador's belt of red silk *bent* the waist without squeezing it, and the bolero of yellow satin covered with black chenille, fringed with velvet pompoms, opened liberally on a naked bust. The belt did not come up to the breasts, perfectly unrestrained upright breasts in their normal place, holding out their hard little tips with the fierce aspect of two reliefs in a breastplate.

Made up in a coarse manner, this woman, whose body could belong to a girl, had a face strangely beautiful and old. The eyes blackened with kohl were too big, too dark, throwing a shadow over all the rest, and the mouth, slashed with red, evoked a painful sensation such as one might feel before a surgical operation. The black hair, held up by a shell comb to shock the gallery, flowered with one single red carnation fixed above the ear, posing there like a reminder of that vermilioned mouth, the apposition of a recent kiss the color of blood. The dancer, whose naked little arms, a child's arms, were extended, whose hands were clenched nervously on castanets, bent over, slowly, and her frail leg, her tiny feet enclosed in black satin, had a kind of shudder, an undulation of the skin, resembling the first tremble of fever.

Missie had come to sit on the floor next to Leon; she was arranging the folds of her Turkish pants, her eyelids lowered.

"You don't recognize her?" she breathed pulling the young man by the sleeve. Hypnotized, the young man was still watching.

"There, it has the same effect, on me too. . . . Yet, it's no mistake, you know, it's Eliante Donalger. *that*!"

"Oh!" murmured the young man, "it's not possible."

"She's worth a few cents, eh?"

"Oh, be quiet!" begged Leon Reille.

The woman danced.

But this dance did not resemble anything familiar either,

anything already seen in the theatre or on the carpets of a salon. It was the living and suffering poem of a body tormented by strange passions. First, the bolero through a continuous and unusual movement of the hips, the lower back and shoulders began to ride up, to descend along the back, it followed the folds of the skin, and these little invisible gestures which made it open, or close over the breasts like the panel of one of those little diptych cupboards, one of those closed paintings where one keeps icons, were curious, if not terrifying, it did not seem natural, and it remained quite simple, but one could not explain why it was abominably troubling. There are some insects who do that a very long time before flying away; they open and close their wings, one sees below transparent elytrons or the very organs of their little life laid bare, and it is all of a sudden charming, light, moving, all of a sudden terrible, it reveals things which must never be known.

Eliante leaned over backwards, and a smile lit up her white face where her eyes put two pits of darkness. One could see her white teeth, beautiful even teeth which seemed to be the teeth of a dead woman. She smiled sadly. The smile became more pronounced while the piano thundered more loudly, a roll of the tambourine caused to shatter, higher up, to scatter in a thousand splinters of glass the notes of the mandolins. It sounded like the immense trampling of panting men, penned into too restricted a space and seeking to escape in order to flee or advance nearer to what they were seeing.

At one point Eliante's bolero nearly jumped off, ripped down the back, and, as she turned, they saw that it was already split and that one could make out the flesh of the shoulders.

"How can she do that?" questioned Leon, crawling on the carpet to get closer, to try to understand.

"Ah! well, it's an invention of the girls from down there . . . street girls, that wouldn't be acceptable in the theatre and . . . it can't be taught, fortunately! Look at her teeth, isn't it funny? You'd think she's going to bite."

"She has admirable teeth!"

"Yes . . . one would think they were false!" concluded Missie.

And the castanets made the dry sound of hail on the windows. Eliante threw herself forward with a supple, enormous leap, and turned, the skirt lifted up to her eyes, all her black body beneath appeared in a leotard, but the leotard let the flesh show through, watershot, one would have said, with a kind of milky sweat, and one ended up seeing, very distinctly, the white flesh of the entire body the way one sees naked legs beneath stockings.

Sometimes, while turning, she would stamp her little right heel and at the same time her elbow on her left knee, dislocating in a strange revolution of lines all the harmony of her person, and more quickly, having turned, placed in profile, her neck stretched out, her eyes calling someone, she would stand up, completely pulled upward by a force, a string which seemed to hold her suspended, her little feet prancing on the spot, trampling mad and frail the St. John's herb, which one sensed burning her soles.[2]

In bigger and bigger leaps, taking off like an uncoiled spring, she moved beyond the green cloth placed on the carpet.

"Aunt," cried Missie, revolted inside because Madame Donalger's breasts were really a bit too much on display, and because Leon, instead of being scandalized, remained decidedly in ecstasy, sobered up or more intoxicated than ever; "Aunt, you're going to sprain something!"

Eliante was smiling, no longer concerned with earth. She was dancing for herself, in a hell she knew well, and did not fear the obstacles.

Louise Frehel, playing, standing up, in front of her

piano, was looking at her with the awe of an artist who sees a rare thing.

On a last chord, she made an imperceptible sign to Leon; he got up and came to her, very worried.

"Throw her the shawl on which you're spread out. It's going to be over soon, and she must not *mess up* that tableau. Missie has forgotten the shawl."

Passively, Leon picked up at random a big black burnous spangled with gold.

"What do I have to do?" he asked Missie in a very low voice.

"Throw it . . . it doesn't matter how! It's really time she cover up, she's too much like a clown."

Leon approached, but he was very afraid.

Eliante seized the end of the burnous and, with a single turn, enveloped herself in it, her fist placed on her hip, causing to jut out under the black veil a straight line, rigid, an iron bar.

"Ah! my dear! my dear!" cried Mademoiselle Frehel. And she came and threw herself madly upon her neck. "It's Spain . . . the real thing! . . . "

"Yes . . . Spain!" repeated Leon, with the air of a beaten dog.

"Aunt, it's horrible! Dancers like that, they should be shot."

Eliante fled into the wings of the screens, bursting with a sickly laughter.

"Madame Donalger," cried Louise Frehel, "don't listen to her . . . she's a child who doesn't know what it's all about."

"We'll kill the dancer!" replied the distant voice of Madame Donalger.

There was a second of real anguish.

She came back, and they let out a cry. She was holding a

jar of makeup, which she had smeared completely down the front of her costume. It formed a torrential sash of dark red from the belt right down to the chenille fringes, and with her two fingers dipped in the bottom of the jar she slit her throat, moved them over her naked breast and traced the path of the blood which spurted in a gush.

"It's horrible!" shouted Missie. "You can see it nauseates us!"

Leon, pale as death, forced a smile.

"Madame, you'll never dance again, will you," he said imperiously.

"No, never again! Excuse me, it's the last whim of my youth which . . . is dying. . . . I'm leaving."

When she returned, she was the grand lady in white, quite proper, and she held out her hands to them.

"My husband used to like this entertainment very much, and it was my Ninaude, the poor negress who was so dirty who had taught me it. It's neither Spanish nor *Caribbean*, it has elements of both, but I'm a little rusty, and I get no pleasure out of dancing now. Things are missing . . . "

She was looking gently at Leon, and she sat down on the swan tuffet.

"My little children," she added fanning herself, "be gay! the dancer is dead."

They all three sat down at her feet, huddled like birds frightened by the storm's wind.

"That's a beautiful costume ruined!" murmured Missie sulking.

"Ah! on the stage of the Opera, in the full light of a grand evening! . . . " repeated Mademoiselle Frehel, shaking her head.

"He had some strange tastes . . . your husband! . . . " muttered Leon, pushing his nails into his palms.

There was no longer any question of trifles.

Someone seemed to have come and placed himself in their midst, without ceremony, and he was taking his share, absorbing all the gaiety.

"We'll have dinner soon, children, soon, and I'll let you go to sleep, after dinner, for we're all tired, aren't we. You, Missie, you're hungry, you're yawning . . . and you, Louise, you have to play again tonight?"

"Yes, an interlude, two pieces on the harp at the Baroness d'Esmont's. One has to get back in the harness!" (She added, caressingly:) "Why were you not an artist, quite simply?"

"Because juggling or dancing, it isn't art . . . it's . . . "

She was going to admit: *it's love*, but she fell silent.

"Tell us a story, madame," breathed Leon, his spirits picking up again, "it will calm us down."

"A Spanish story," said Missie.

Madame Donalger stroked their three hands united in hers.

"Ah! the good little children, who could waltz and who want stories! . . . Well, once upon a time there was a nun in the heart of a dark Spanish convent, a nun burned by all the fires of hell and yet who believed in God. This nun of the devil was most beautiful, a tall brunette with the lightest shadow of a moustache on her lip. She was so bored that one night she slipped over the convent walls; but before going over the walls of this convent, she had gone into the chapel to make herself a beautiful outfit. She had cut a doublet out of a chasuble of gold, put on violet slippers and took the lace from the altar of the Virgin, then also the strong sword decorated with precious stones of Saint Michael Archangel. She roamed the world in this disguise, turned Spain upside down, taking daughters from their mothers and wives from their husbands, under the name of . . . *Don Juan*."

"What?" said Leon jumping. "And no one, neither the daughters, nor the wives . . . "

"Certain estates have their graces, sir! She was wearing the altar decorations, and God, to punish her for her sacrilege, had changed her into . . . a man. But she died a *woman* and repentant, in front of My Lady the Virgin, whom she hadn't been able to seduce or wanted to offend."

"So be it!" growled Leon.

"You know," concluded Eliante, "that this legend exists in a book written by a former monk, an inquisitor,[3] I suppose, wanting to excuse in advance the *Don Juans* to come, and it really is only this story which could permit the creation of the type of all fickle seducers, for *Don Juan*, the first of that name, the king of Spain, died of love for his legitimate wife, and *Don Juan* of Austria, the generous, the conqueror, was a pious person much more shot through with glory than with love. Me, I would willingly believe that, to be the passionate person *par excellence*, one must have a heart as close to the devil as to God, that's to say be a proud man or a woman . . . dreaming of the infinite! Now, my children, let's have dinner! Here is Uncle Donalger returning, I hear his carriage . . . "

They had dinner. The old diplomat poured, in glasses of pink crystal tinted with gold, wine dating, he claimed, from his birth, and everyone drank with their own particular devotion.

Missie seemed mad, tried to lose herself in childish prattling, a little intoxicated already.

Louise Frehel was talking music, apparently irritated to leave the house where she felt so at home.

Eliante was quiet, dreaming perhaps about Spain.

Leon was quiet . . . thinking about the night.

That night . . .

He feared some mundane complication. Mademoiselle

Frehel asking him to accompany her, but Eliante had foreseen that. She offered her own carriage to the girl, whom she knew to be poor.

Leon took his leave, very serious, absolutely sober, his heart beating, and he returned via the garden one hour later, the mysterious little garden, of which he found the gate open.

Eliante Donalger was waiting for him all white, on the steps, all white and fantastically bathed in moon.

"Come in," she said, "the house is asleep, and the lights are out. Come quickly and close the doors tight."

She spoke simply.

In the green dining room, one seemed to be in the water of a warm spring, and it was fragrant with island fruit.

Eliante held out her hand to him, and continued mouth to mouth:

"I've done everything my master ordered. This very day I sent a copy of the deed which divides my fortune between Missie and her uncle. I'm poor, poorer than the little artist who went, this evening, to earn her bread by making others waltz. The house no longer belongs to me. I've given it to someone outright with everything agreeable it contains. But I smashed the wax statues and the collection of ivories so that *the children* should not be scandalized . . . I remain naked . . . in my dress, my only dress and my black leotard . . . my juggler's outfit, my last costume. . . . Tomorrow morning, I'll leave . . . "

"Where for, my God?"

"I'll go and return to my country, the kingdom of my dreams! The heat!"

"And me?"

"You'll stay here!"

"Never! I'll follow you . . . "

"No! Accept tonight, the only night of love possible between us, the one which must never end, for I'll leave you an unforgettable souvenir. I'm a big coquette? So be it! I want my wishes respected."

He pressed her madly in his arms.

"Enough! Enough! No macabre juggling. I want you, and if you want me, you can have no other wishes than mine. I'm the master, you won't leave, I fully take it upon myself to prevent you. Go ahead of me to show me where your bed is . . . and be quiet!"

"Will you at least allow me time to take off my dress?"

"I won't grant you a minute . . . I'll follow you."

He followed her.

In the large closed bedroom, everything was so dark that he had the dizzying feeling of throwing himself into a chasm.

And he had to get his bearings for a moment, let go of her wrist.

A horrible anguish gripped the young man.

"Eliante! talk to me . . . Eliante, where are you? . . . I forbid you to be quiet, at the moment, I want to hear your voice."

"I'm here, my beloved," answered the already distant voice, "I'm taking off my dress . . . in front of my bed. . . . Come . . . "

And he perceived a slight noise of rustling silk.

Really, it was no longer making love! It was almost committing a crime, but having torn off his own clothes in mad gestures, he rushed toward the bed.

Finally, she was there, alive, and she embraced him with the strange shiver of a child who is afraid.

. . . The young male, tired, half opened his eyes, stretched nervously in the lace and silks of this strange bed, in the shape of an egg. He turned over, letting slide the torso of she who was still sleeping deeply at his side.

What was this light which was penetrating through the topaz window panes?

Dawn or fire?

He lowered his eyelids again, sighed, raised them once again, sighed more heavily. No, he was dreaming!

He was dreaming that Eliante's bedroom was lit up for one of those pretty gay parties she knew how to give to her *little children*, men!

He was dreaming that he could see her, her, the unusual woman whose cold virgin's flesh could not be moved by caresses, whose heart did not blossom in ardent words beneath the beating of an ardent breast . . . that he could see her juggling . . .

Always her juggler's knives! Her damned knives which she dared to prefer to him!

Did they bite better?

In a bad mood, the young man, tired and naked, pulled up the sheets. He thought confusedly that she would not be able to jump out of this bed without having to pass over his body.

And that thought woke him up more . . . because the bed was in the middle of the room. He looked at everything.

But no, his dream continued. It is very difficult to shake off a nightmare of love.

He saw Eliante again in her juggler outfit. She came forward, in a glory of gold, holding by the point the five swords of pain.

She was approaching the bed perhaps to kill him?

Decidedly, it had to be the perfume of the island fruit of which she took unfair advantage, which made him drunk, gave him a headache, saturated his skin and made him all clammy.

And also that smell of wild animal, the dominant smell

of the room, of the temple, that musty smell of negro fat!"

Ah! He was breathing fire. He wanted to wake up, to check that she was indeed still there, asleep, and not in the process of juggling in front of their bed . . .

. . . She was approaching, with tiny steps, so beautiful in her dark costume all sparkling with stars and her fierce warrior's helmet, her black hair was shining like steel. Her staring pupils were flaming, making her ivory face, her red mouth with the accentuated dimples, more tragic.

And Leon Reille, yawning a little, propped himself up on his elbow, watching her juggle without much surprise, because, this nightmare, he had had it very often, and it seemed natural to him to find her at the same time quite naked laying near him, and standing up in front of him, juggling in a black silk leotard.

He only understood completely when *the other* Eliante, woken in her turn by the clicking of the knives, let out a shrill cry, a cry of unspeakable childish terror. Then he jumped, tried to escape from Missie's arms, which clung onto him, in panic.

"Eliante! Eliante!" he groaned twisting in pain and shame. "A knife for me . . . I don't want to live any longer! A knife for me . . . "

Eliante, still impassive, put one knee on the ground and raising her inspired eyes, joyful with a supernatural joy, threw very high her handsome juggler's knife . . . but instead of pulling back her head, presenting her chest, she *changed the routine*, stretched out her throat. The knife, heavier, coming from higher, planted itself straight in, and her powerful little fingers drove it in, pushed with all their might, clenched on the ebony handle.

The woman slipped backwards. A purple wave drowned the pale mask . . . her last makeup . . .

. . . In a faint, mouth to mouth, the two children had

fallen back on their nuptial bed, indissolubly united, now, by the same sacred horror.

Less than a year later, Marie Chamerot could think that her husband would forget, for he had smiled as he kissed the little girl who had just been born.

"You'll love her, our child?" said the new mother, all happy. "She'll be pretty . . . "

"Yes," answered Leon, "I hope she'll have *her eyes*, the eyes of dream."

FIN

Explanatory Notes

Chapter One

1. *L'Animale*, "The Animal," was the title of a novel Rachilde published in 1893 (Paris: H. Simonis Empis), in which the heroine, Laure Lordès, has pronounced animalistic qualities.

2. According to Michelet, being carried off on a black horse is the fate of a witch (see Catherine Clément, "The Guilty One" in *The Newly Born Woman*, Minneapolis: University of Minnesota Press, 1986, 5). Rachilde's depiction of Eliante draws on this tradition of female disruption to create a figure who blends both witch and hysteric.

3. Leon's sneering remark is no doubt a reference to the fact that Eliante is the name of a secondary character in Molière's play *The Misanthrope*. Eliante is an emblem of good sense and modesty, having a "solid and sincere heart" (act 1, scene 1), in contrast to the dazzling heroine, the coquette Célimène. The importance of this contrast emerges in the accusations of coquetry levelled at Eliante in *The Juggler*. Perhaps also relevant to Rachilde's choice of this name for her heroine is Eliante's long speech in act 2, scene 4 of Molière's play, where she opposes the

hero Alceste's claim that true love means not pardoning the loved one's faults. Eliante maintains instead that love makes people blind to the shortcomings of the "object" of their passion:

> . . . l'on voit les amants vanter toujours leur choix;
> Jamais leur passion n'y voit rien de blâmable,
> Et dans l'objet aimé tout leur devient aimable.
>
> One sees lovers always praise their choice
> Their passion never sees any cause for blame
> And in the love object everything becomes lovable

The heroine of *The Juggler* also denies that there can be any "blame" attached to her passion, and finds that objects become lovable when they are loved.

Although Rachilde apparently was not an admirer of Molière (see the letter from Jarry to Rachilde in *Organographes du Cymbalum Pataphysicum*, no. 18, September 8, 1982, 35), the allusion to Classical French drama underscores the dramatic aspects of *The Juggler*.

4. It was a well-known fact that Rachilde did not like dancing. Although she met her future husband, Alfred Vallette, at a dance, he wrote to her (presumably in 1885): "You write like other people go to the ball, for fun (and you don't dance since you've decided that that is an inappropriate form of exercise)" (my translation). Rachilde published Vallette's early letters to her in *Le Roman d'un homme sérieux*, "The Novel of a Serious Man" (Paris: Mercure de France, 1944) using the same epithet—"serious"—that Eliante continually applies to Leon.

5. Such echoes of ennui caused Rachilde to be dubbed "Mademoiselle Baudelaire" (in an article of that title, by Maurice Barrès, in *Les Chroniques*, February 1887, 77–79).

6. Born in 1860, Rachilde turned forty in 1900, the year of *The Juggler*'s publication.

7. Although Rachilde was a member of the club Les Hydropathes, she drank only water all her life. It was a fact often noted by Rachilde herself and one strongly associated with her by friends and acquaintances, who also refer to it. Rachilde's insistence on this aspect of Eliante's character suggests a strong autobiographical element in her depiction.

Chapter Two

1. The Bullier Ball, also known as the Closerie des Lilas, was a popular dance hall frequented by the young, especially law and medical students. It was at the Bal Bullier that Rachilde met Alfred Vallette in 1885. They were married four years later.

2. Slang for a disagreeable person.

3. Georges Dieulafoy (1839–1911) was the author, in 1880, of a pathology manual (*Manuel de pathologie interne*) which became the "bible" of medical students for thirty years.

4. It was well known to all Rachilde's contemporaries that she kept open house on Tuesdays, and her salon was very popular. Among the regular guests were those associated with the symbolist movement and the *Mercure de France* (Rémy de Gourmont, Marcel Schwob, Pierre Louys, Alfred Jarry, Pierre Quillard, Paul Fort, Ferdinand Hérold, Louis Dumur, Jean Lorrain).

Chapter Three

1. On his first visit to Eliante's house in chapter 1, Leon had entered via the garden, but on this occasion he arrives via the courtyard. The terms "côté jardin" and "côté cour" (garden side and courtyard side, respectively) are used to indicate the direction of each subsequent visit to Eliante's house, culminating with a visit via the garden in the final chapter. The terms are borrowed from seventeenth-century classical French drama, and thus add to the novel's theatrical aspect, but the opposition also corresponds to a public/private distinction. When arriving via the garden, Leon sees an intimate side of Eliante, while visits via the courtyard are public, social occasions.

2. Yvette Guilbert (Emma Laure Esther, 1865–1944) was a popular singer, immortalized in Toulouse-Lautrec's portraits. In 1912, Rachilde dedicated her book *Son Printemps* ("Her Springtime") to Guilbert with the words: "To Yvette Guilbert, so that she may light a candle, with a tall and pure flame, in the inferno of artistic life."

3. Rachilde was portrayed as a mouse in Léo Paillet's *Dans la ménagerie littéraire*, "In the Literary Menagerie" (Paris: Baudinière, 1925). Rodents were also among Rachilde's favorite pets, as many

friends noted, including Colette. In *De ma fenêtre*, "From My Window," she recorded: "I had the pleasure of approaching the rats that Rachilde used to tame. The novelist held the character of the rat in such esteem that it supplanted other familiar animals for her. White and beige, brown, some taupe-gray, lustrous, her five or six rats would freely leave and re-enter a cage, the door of which often remained open, like domesticated parrots. 'Rats are to my liking,' Madame Rachilde used to say, 'they have strong attachments and a proud nature.' Indeed, they heard her words and calls with joy and obdience, and, like her, they had eyes that shone unflinchingly, and sharp, unbroken teeth." See Colette, *Oeuvres complètes* 10 (Paris: Flammarion, 1973), 72. (I am indebted to Lynne Huffer for drawing my attention to this passage.)

4. Pierre-Louis Duval (1811–1870) began as a butcher in Paris but went on to open twelve "economical" restaurants called "Bouillons Duval" because they originally served only bouillon (beef broth) and boiled beef. Later, in response to public demand, the menu was enlarged, and the low-priced restaurants continued to enjoy popularity into the twentieth century.

5. As as army officer, Rachilde's father, Joseph Eymery, had fought in the 1870 Franco-Prussian war. Although not wounded, he returned home deaf and pockmarked, having contracted smallpox while a prisoner of war in Hamburg.

6. Rachilde had some personal experience of arranged marriages. When she was only fourteen, she was engaged by her parents to an officer of her father's acquaintance. To avoid the marriage, Rachilde made a halfhearted attempt at suicide by throwing herself into a pond.

7. Mauve was Rachilde's favorite color, and it became the color of the cover of the *Mercure de France*.

8. The fabrication of liqueurs seems to be a hallmark of Rachilde's heroines. This passage is echoed in a later novel, *Madame de Lydone, assassin* (Paris: Ferenczi, 1929), in which the heroine also makes violet liqueur.

9. These prophetic words could be taken as a manifesto for Rachilde's own life, and anticipate the scandalized gossip she provoked in later life when she continued to lead an active social life. Claude Dauphiné, in particular, describes her "folle vieillese," and quotes the report of the concierge at the Mercure de France: "The frightening thing is to see Vallette let her run around everywhere, at night until four o'clock

in the morning, with all these young people of rather equivocal appearance." See Claude Dauphiné, *Rachilde: femme de lettres, 1900* (Périgueux: Pierre Fanlac, 1985), 129.

Chapter Five

1. The phrase "ironie sanglante" (literally, "bleeding irony"), with its pun on "ironie cinglante" (stinging irony), obviously appealed to Rachilde; she had used it as the title of a novel published in 1891. Moreover, it is characteristic both of Rachilde's punning style and her tendency to rework stock phrases and ideas over a long period.

2. The topos is a favorite one for Rachilde. In the last book she ever published, her memoires *Quand j'étais jeune*, "When I Was Young" (Paris: Mercure de France, 1947), she recalls her first visit to the actress Sarah Bernhardt, some seventy years previously. Guests received a somewhat bizarre reception, and Rachilde's vivid desciption includes the detail of the front steps covered, despite the rain, by "a Smyrna carpet the terrible color of blood" (44).

3. Eliante's characteristic dimples were the subject of frequent references in earlier versions of *The Juggler*. Although the metaphor occurs less often in this text, it continues to recall Eliante's relationship to writing: her body is itself a text, while the source of verbal communication is set apart by parentheses.

4. Rachilde's father had been disfigured by smallpox while a prisoner of war. This similarity, combined with the fact that mauve—the color of the wallet in which his portrait is kept—was also Rachilde's favorite color, suggests that the portrait of Henri Donalger owes something to Colonel Eymery. Perhaps Eliante's attempts to free herself from the guilt and paralysing love for her dead husband, a relationship presented as verging on an obsession, represents Rachilde's own attempts to exorcise the memories of her father and their inhibiting power.

5. Eliante's description of the path to passion evokes another allegory, Plato's allegory of the cave. Here the path which ascends from the cave of shadowy illusions to the light of truth is, in the words of Luce Irigaray, "full of traps, it is rocky and rugged, it can wound, tear, cut" (*Speculum of the Other Woman*, translated by Gillian C. Gill, Ithaca, N.Y.: Cornell University Press, 1985, 283).

Chapter Six

1. "My lady ascends her tower," a line from the popular song "Marlbrouk s'en va-t-en guerre" (Marlborough is off to the war), said to date from the early eighteenth century. The verse continues "as high as she can go," echoed in Leon's next line.

Chapter Seven

1. Earlier editions of *The Juggler* specify that "Colmans" is not the guest's real name, despite his affinity for mustard. Instead, he had acquired this nickname "because of an old joke that no one remembered."

2. Perhaps an allusion to Alfred Jarry's play *Ubu Roi*, first performed in 1896. Rachilde had been instrumental in getting this play performed.

3. The mistake was especially easy to make in the case of jugglers (*jongleurs*). In addition to acrobatics, composing, and entertaining with songs and poems, female *jongleurs* "were routinely assumed to engage in prostitution," at least in the Middle Ages. See Joseph J. Duggan, "The Epic," in *A New History of French Literature* edited by Denis Hollier (Cambridge, Mass.: Harvard University Press, 1989), 18–23.

Chapter Eight

1. "Je vous aime. Je t'aime." English has no equivalent to convey the transition from the formal "vous" form of address to the intimate "tu" form. Eliante first uses the informal "tu" in chapter 5, but both she and Leon alternate usage many times, marking the transitions between periods of intimacy and distance.

2. Eliante is here referring to her brother-in-law, but these generous sentiments also echo those of Rachilde herself. In the 1880s she gave refuge to the ailing poet Verlaine, vacating her apartment for him, and she and Vallette would be similarly unstinting in their generous support of Alfred Jarry.

3. The responsibilities of a "trottin" (literally, "one who trots")

would be similar to those of the modern "gopher," but the French term conveys more than a job description, being a term of moral and intellectual judgement.

4. In *Pourquoi je ne suis pas féministe*, "Why I am Not a Feminist" (Paris: Les Editions de France, 1928), Rachilde cites (among others) Teresa of Avila as an example of a women stricken by "the heavenly malady" (49). The same figure is analyzed by Jacques Lacan in his *Le Séminaire, Livre xx: Encore* (Paris: Seuil, 1975), where he discusses Bernini's sculpture of St. Teresa as a representation of *jouissance*.

5. Perhaps a reference to the Terror of 1793, and also to Victor Hugo's novel *Quatre-vingt-treize* (*1793*). Rachilde had great respect for Hugo, who had encouraged her literary ambitions before she ever reached Paris.

6. Rachilde here anticipates the question that would be posed by Freud in his letter to Marie Bonaparte: "Was will das Weib," usually translated as "what do women want" (see Ernest Jones, *Sigmund Freud: Life and Work*, vol. 2. London, 1955, 468). Rachilde's formulation, however, being in the form of a statement and not a question, also anticipates the postmodern response that women *cannot* know what they want.

Chapter Nine

1. The panther was the subject of one of Rachilde's plays, and many of her contemporaries chose to see a self-portrait in her depiction of this animal.

2. According to French law, women always legally retain their unmarried name, even after marriage.

3. Rachilde was in fact born in 1860. However, there was confusion, even among her friends, about her date of birth, so that even her obituary in *Le Monde* gives it as 1862.

4. This rank of nobility was something of an obsession for Rachilde, perhaps because her father was the illegitimate son of a marquis. Rachilde herself dressed up as a marquise for a fancy dress ball just before her marriage to Alfred Vallette, and he addresses her as "marquise" in his correspondence of this period. The marquise is also a com-

mon figure in Rachilde's fiction, with the "Marquise de Sade" being perhaps the best known. Both because of her aristocratic ancestry and through temperament, Rachilde was drawn to emblems of the *ancien régime*, and seems to have felt a certain spiritual affinity with the figure of the *grande dame*, the gracious noblewoman. Other traces of this predilection—in the form of references to Louis XIV, XV, and XVI—appeared in earlier versions of *The Juggler*, but were later edited out.

Chapter Ten

1. Again, the transition here is from the formal "vous" to the more intimate "tu,' a nuance impossible to capture in English. See chapter 8, note 1.

Chapter Twelve

1. A line from a popular song: "We'll go to the woods no more, the laurels have been cut down." *Les Lauriers sont coupés* is also the title of a novel by Edouard Dujardin. It was originally published in the *Revue Indépendente*, a symbolist journal edited by Dujardin from 1886 to 1889. It was subsequently reissued by the Mercure de France in 1897 (the year in which *The Juggler* is set), and was reviewed by Rachilde in the August edition of the *Mercure de France*. Dujardin's novel may have influenced Rachilde, as it depicts a man torn bewteen a conscious ideal of platonic love and somewhat less conscious carnal desire. In addition, it is the first example of a novel in the form of an interior monologue, and James Joyce cited it as an influence in the composition of *Ulysses*. *Les Lauriers sont coupés*, like *The Juggler*, is therefore an important example of the symbolist roots of modernism.

2. St John's herb (eupatorium), also known as Devilfuge, was used to dispel witches and demons. The cult of St. John incorporated many mystical elements from pre-Christian tradition, and St. John's Eve (24 June) is the occasion for numerous magical rituals. See Hilderic Friend, *Flower Lore*, first printed in England in 1884 and reprinted in Rockport, MA by Para Research in 1981. Friend's encyclopedic collection of folklore suggests: "It seems as though almost every plant which

has any association with St. John has also at some time or another been credited with the possession of supernatural powers, both among ourselves [in Britain], and especially on the Continent." (75).

3. Rachilde counted both a defrocked priest and a Spanish Grand Inquisitor among her ancestors. She also described her father as a "Don Juan" in her memoirs *Quand j'étais jeune*.